F
STR   Strickland, Brad
        The tower at the
        end of the world

DATE DUE

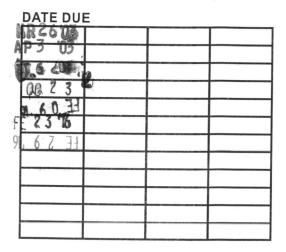

Read Across America
2003
Mrs. Phelp's
Class

V⁰³

The Tower at
the End of the World

BY BRAD STRICKLAND
(based on John Bellairs's characters)

The Tower at the End of the World
The Beast under the Wizard's Bridge
The Wrath of the Grinning Ghost
The Specter From the Magician's Museum
The Bell, the Book, and the Spellbinder
The Hand of the Necromancer

BOOKS BY JOHN BELLAIRS
COMPLETED BY BRAD STRICKLAND

The Doom of the Haunted Opera
The Drum, the Doll, and the Zombie
The Vengeance of the Witch-Finder
The Ghost in the Mirror

BOOKS BY JOHN BELLAIRS

The Mansion in the Mist
The Secret of the Underground Room
The Chessmen of Doom
The Trolley to Yesterday
The Lamp from the Warlock's Tomb
The Eyes of the Killer Robot
The Revenge of the Wizard's Ghost
The Spell of the Sorcerer's Skull
The Dark Secret of Weatherend
The Mummy, the Will, and the Crypt
The Curse of the Blue Figurine
The Treasure of Alpheus Winterborn
The Letter, the Witch, and the Ring
The Figure in the Shadows
The House with a Clock in Its Walls

John Bellairs's Lewis Barnavelt in

THE TOWER
AT THE END
OF THE WORLD

A sequel to
THE HOUSE WITH A CLOCK IN ITS WALLS

BY

BRAD STRICKLAND

Frontispiece
by S. D. Schindler

Dial Books for Young Readers
New York

Published by Dial Books for Young Readers
A division of Penguin Putnam Inc.
345 Hudson Street
New York, New York 10014

3 5 7 9 10 8 6 4 2

Library of Congress Cataloging-in-Publication Data
Strickland, Brad.
The tower at the end of the world / by Brad Strickland ;
frontispiece by S. D. Schindler.
p. cm.
Summary: Lewis and Rose Rita battle Ishmael Izard,
the son of the evil magician who tried to destroy the world
with the Doomsday Clock.
ISBN 0-8037-2620-1
[1. Magic—Fiction. 2. Supernatural—Fiction.
3. Wizards—Fiction.] I. Title.

PZ7.S916703 To 2001
[Fic]—dc21   00-065889

In memory of three
who will be forever missed,

John Bellairs
Frank Bellairs
Edward Gorey

The Tower at
the End of the World

CHAPTER ONE

Lewis Barnavelt closed his book with a snap. He popped the last of his chocolate-covered peppermints into his mouth. He didn't chew it, but let the sweet chocolate melt on his tongue, releasing the cool mint taste. Then he sat in the lawn chair under the old chestnut tree in front of 100 High Street with his chin in his hand. He wasn't smiling. In fact, he looked decidedly gloomy.

There was no obvious reason. It was a warm, breezy June day in the 1950's. School had recently ended, and Lewis had a whole summer of freedom ahead, days when he could do just about anything you could do in the town of New Zebedee, Michigan. And he looked forward to nights when he and his uncle, Jonathan Barnavelt, could haul out their telescope and stargaze in the backyard.

But none of that helped much at the moment. All Lewis

could feel then was grumpy, grouchy, and irritable. It didn't even help when he heard his friend Rose Rita Pottinger call out to him from the street: "Hi, Lewis! What have you got on? Your mind?"

Lewis made a face. He got enough ridicule at school, he thought, and he didn't need Rose Rita's ribbing, even if it was good-humored.

Lewis was a heavyset boy of about thirteen, with a round moon face and hair that he slicked back with oil and parted in the center. He was anything but athletic. When the kids played baseball or softball, Lewis was always the last one chosen, if he was chosen at all. He had always been timid about getting hurt, and he didn't dare try to join in the rough-and-tumble football games the other kids played in the fall. And though he could usually take gentle teasing from Rose Rita or from his uncle or Mrs. Zimmermann, their next-door neighbor, today his mood was just too dismal. So he stood up with a dramatic sigh and said, "I was about to go take a nap."

Rose Rita pushed open the wrought-iron gate in front of Lewis's house, which was a three-story stone mansion. She grinned and said, "Well, I think you'll change your tune when you hear my news."

"I doubt it," said Lewis.

Rose Rita tilted her head to one side. She was somewhat taller than Lewis, and she was skinny, with long, straight dark hair. She wore big round glasses and looked sort of gawky and clumsy, though she could run like the wind and could outpitch almost any boy in a game of baseball. "Come on, don't be a Gloomy Gus. What's the matter with you?"

Lewis sniffed. "Nothing." He shrugged. "Just bored, I guess." That wasn't the whole truth. In fact, Lewis, who loved to read, had just finished the very last novel about Dr. Fu-Manchu. He was a Chinese master criminal, whom the author Sax Rohmer described as having a forehead like Shakespeare's and a face like Satan's. In every book the evil Fu-Manchu's plots failed at the last minute because the criminal was beaten by his nemesis, a stalwart British detective named Nayland Smith. Now that Lewis had finished reading *The Shadow of Fu-Manchu*, he realized he had no more of the adventures to discover, and that made him feel cranky.

Rose Rita stared at him for a minute. Everything was silent except for the rustling of the chestnut leaves in the breeze. Then she asked, "Where's your uncle?"

"Out back," said Lewis. "He decided to do some flower gardening."

Rose Rita's eyebrows shot up. Jonathan Barnavelt had attended an agricultural college when he was young, but then he had inherited a pot of money from his grandfather. Every year he planted a vegetable patch in the rear of the backyard, but usually he was too lazy to plant any flowers. "Let's go see him," said Rose Rita. "This involves him too."

Lewis was interested despite himself. In a way, he still wanted to brood about not having any more Sax Rohmer books to read. But something about Rose Rita's manner made him curious. He dropped his book on the lawn chair, but he kept his tone gruff. "Okay, I'll go with you."

They walked around back. Jonathan Barnavelt knelt beside a flower bed. He was wearing tan wash pants, a blue work shirt, and his red vest. He also wore brown cotton work gloves, and he was wielding a rusty trowel as he set out the last of some colorful petunias.

"Hello, you two!" he boomed with a big smile as Rose Rita and Lewis came around the corner of the house. He got to his feet, dusted off the knees of his trousers, and peeled off the gloves. Then he stood with his hands on his hips, admiring his handiwork. "There! Every year Florence kids me about not growing anything but sweet corn and tomatoes in my yard. I guess this will show her! I mean to have some prize petunias this year." He wiped sweat from his forehead with a big red bandanna, leaving a brownish smudge of soil. "That's hot work. I'm thirsty for some nice cold lemonade. Care to join me?"

Lewis had to fight hard to hold on to his grumpy mood. Ever since his parents had died in a tragic auto accident, Lewis had lived with his uncle in the big house on High Street. Though there were still times when he felt lonesome for his mom and dad, he liked the arrangement a great deal. Jonathan Barnavelt was a big man with a pot belly and a bushy red beard. He loved to laugh, he loved to eat, and best of all, he loved magic. He was a sorcerer who could create marvelous magical illusions out of thin air. Because of that and his great sense of humor, living with him was never dull. However, Lewis was determined not to be jollied along, and so he just grunted and shrugged.

Jonathan didn't seem to notice. He led the way back to the house and into the kitchen, where he opened the refrigerator and took out a frosty pitcher of lemonade. He poured three tall glasses and handed them around.

"A toast," he said. "To warm weather, plenty of rain, and a good growing season!" He clinked glasses with Rose Rita, but Lewis didn't join in. After a long sip of lemonade Jonathan said, "I guess Lewis is in a sour mood today, so this drink should just about suit him."

Lewis frowned. "I just don't feel much like talking. I don't know why everybody's picking on me today."

"Nobody's picking on you," replied Rose Rita. "In fact, I came over with a terrific invitation for you. And for your uncle and Mrs. Zimmermann too. Could we call her over?"

Jonathan shook his head. "We could if she were home, but Florence is out of town until this afternoon. She had some legal business to settle over in Homer."

Lewis felt a twinge of concern. Their neighbor Mrs. Florence Zimmermann was a fabulous cook, a sympathetic and helpful friend, and a witch. Not an evil witch, but a friendly, cheerful, wrinkly-faced good witch whose magic, as Uncle Jonathan always admitted, was much stronger than his own. "What's wrong, Uncle Jonathan?" asked Lewis. "Is somebody suing Mrs. Zimmermann?"

Looking astonished at the very idea, Jonathan said, "Suing Haggy Face? Of course not! You know how she's always crabbed about the old fishing dock next to her property on Lyon Lake, the one that she says is a public menace because the owner never repairs it. Well, she's said for years that she was going to buy the ramshackle old thing from the owner and have it torn down, and now she's finally done it. She's signing the deed today, that's all. So, Rose Rita, if you want us all together for your invitation, you'll just have to wait."

Rose Rita was almost bouncing in her chair. "But I can't wait! It's too exciting. I'll tell you and Lewis, but you'll have to promise not to talk to Mrs. Zimmermann before I get a chance."

Now Lewis was certainly intrigued. He knew all about the close friendship between Rose Rita and Mrs. Zimmermann. It was almost as if they were sisters, if one sister could be in her teens and the other about seventy. "Okay, I promise," said Lewis, and Jonathan added his promise as well.

Behind the lenses of her spectacles, Rose Rita's eyes were dancing. "You know my grampa Galway."

Jonathan Barnavelt looked perplexed. "Of course I know Albert. What about him?"

Albert Galway, Rose Rita's grandfather, was a tall, bald old man who was something of a character in New Zebedee. Though Mr. Galway always told people he was almost ninety, Lewis had recently learned from Rose Rita that he really was only eighty-one. Still, that was a long life, and in that long life Mr. Galway had done lots of things. He had run away from home at the age of sixteen and had joined the Navy for four years. Then he had returned to New Zebedee, finished his schooling, and had become a construction worker, a pretty good photographer and artist, and then an architect. He had rejoined the Navy twice, once for two years during World War I and then another four-year hitch in the Depression, and had traveled all over the world. He still loved to roam around, and he had a passionate interest in gadgets and gizmos. "What about your grampa?" repeated Lewis.

"He's going to be up at a place near Porcupine Bay all summer," Rose Rita told him. "An old Navy buddy of his is off in Australia racing a yacht, and he's asked my grampa to house-sit at his mansion. It's on an island in Lake Superior, with a sailboat. And Grampa Galway says we can all come up and visit him!"

Lewis's heart thumped. A sailboat! Now, that was interesting. But then he gulped. Lewis was a real worrywart, always imagining the worst, and he thought about all the possible dangers. Porcupine Bay was on the wild Upper Peninsula of Michigan, a curving finger of land that bent out to the east between Lake Superior to the north and Lake Michigan to the south. Lewis had been there once or twice, and sometimes he read stories in the newspapers about marauding bears, dangerous lightning storms, and forest fires in the wilderness. What would happen if they were all out on a sailboat and a bad storm blew up? He could picture them falling into the cold waters, floundering and splashing, screaming for help as one by one they drowned.

But Jonathan Barnavelt looked delighted. "That sounds great! I know Albert's had lots of experience at the helm of a sailing boat, and he's always entertaining to talk to. I'm ready to go right now! How about you, Lewis?"

His uncle's enthusiasm forced a smile onto Lewis's face.

He swallowed the cold, sour lump of fear that had risen in his throat. "It sounds pretty good," he admitted. "I guess it would be fun."

Rose Rita gave him an exasperated glance. "Of course it'll be fun! We'll get to explore, and we can pretend that we're the crew of Sir Francis Drake's *Golden Hind,* bound on a voyage around the world! We can have picnics and go swimming and fishing. Maybe we can even camp out overnight on one of the islands up there. That'll be better than sitting around with our noses stuck in books all summer!"

"Hey!" objected Lewis.

Jonathan patted Lewis on the shoulder. "There's nothing wrong with loving to read. Lewis, I've got a suggestion. We'll swing by my favorite used-book store over in Ann Arbor before we go, and you can stock up on adventure stories. And I'll even spring for a whole case of peppermint patties!"

Lewis nodded, and the smile that he had been fighting off curved itself across his face. "That sounds great." He loved to eat candy while he read, and most of his books had chocolate-colored fingerprints on the corners of the pages. "Okay, I'm in. When do we tell Mrs. Zimmermann?"

"*We* don't," Rose Rita shot back. "I do that all by myself. I want it to be my surprise!"

Rose Rita stayed for lunch, and after a round of hot roast-beef sandwiches and some potato salad, she helped Lewis clean up. Not long after that, Mrs. Zimmermann came rattling along High Street in Bessie, her purple Plymouth, and Rose Rita and Lewis ran over to her house to give her the news. She laughed at Rose Rita's excitement as they sat on the purple sofa in her living room, under the oil painting of a purple dragon done for Mrs. Zimmermann years and years earlier by the great French painter Odilon Redon. Mrs. Zimmermann's favorite color was purple, and she made no bones about surrounding herself with it. She wore baggy purple dresses, and even the toilet paper in her bathrooms was purple.

"My heavens!" she exclaimed when Rose Rita had finished. She adjusted her gold-rimmed spectacles on her nose, her eyes gleaming with good humor. "Here I was thinking this was going to be a quiet stay-at-home kind of summer, and now this. Rose Rita, I would be delighted to accept your invitation. Thank Albert for me, and let me know when we're going. Now, who's for some chocolate-chip cookies?"

Lewis licked his lips. His uncle was a rotten cook who could just about manage to turn out an edible sandwich or a hamburger, but Mrs. Zimmermann could dish up delicious meals and scrumptious treats. For half an hour they sat at her kitchen table, gobbling fresh crunchy cookies and slurping tall glasses of milk. When they had finished, Mrs. Zimmermann said, "Why not take Weird Beard a dozen cookies? If he's going to be sailing and fishing and hiking, he'll need to keep his strength up!" She packed the cookies in a paper lunch bag, and Lewis and Rose Rita headed over to Lewis's house.

They barged into the living room. The TV set, a Zenith Stratocaster with a perfectly round screen, like a porthole, was on. Lewis recognized *House Party*, an afternoon show that his uncle sometimes watched. But no one was in the living room.

"Uncle Jonathan?" called Lewis. When no answer came, he gave Rose Rita an uneasy glance. "I wonder where he is."

Rose Rita knew how Lewis could work himself up over nothing. "Probably he's gone upstairs," she suggested in a reasonable tone. "Maybe he needed a shower after all his work on the flower beds."

But Jonathan wasn't on the second floor or even on the unused third floor of the house. The two friends came back downstairs with Lewis feeling more and more tense. It wasn't like his uncle to walk out of a room and leave the TV set or the radio playing. They went toward the kitchen, and Lewis noticed that the door to the cellar was ajar. Then he remembered that Uncle Jonathan stored his fishing tackle down there, in a kind of cupboard built into the wall near the furnace. "I'll bet he's getting out his rods and reels," he said with relief in his voice. "Come on."

Lewis stepped onto the cellar stairs and looked down into darkness. Surely his uncle would have turned on the light. He fumbled for the switch and clicked it. Nothing happened. "Uncle Jonathan?" Lewis called down into the darkness. "Are you there?"

"I don't like this," mumbled Rose Rita. "It isn't like him to disappear with no warning."

"Get the flashlight from the junk drawer in the kitchen," Lewis told her. She hurried away.

Lewis stood on the top step, his heart hammering. Had

the lightbulb burned out? Had Jonathan started down to change it and tripped in the dark? Was he hurt?

Soon Rose Rita was back with the flashlight. Lewis switched it on and sent its bright beam downward. The big yellow oval of light traced the steps, then moved slowly over the concrete basement floor. It came to rest on something long and tan.

His uncle's leg!

Lewis hurried downstairs. Jonathan Barnavelt lay motionless on his stomach, his hands flung out. His face was turned away from Lewis, and for a terrible, wrenching moment, Lewis thought he might be dead. Then the fallen figure stirred and groaned.

Lewis shined the flashlight on Rose Rita, who was standing halfway down the steps. "He's knocked out!" he yelled. "Go get Mrs. Zimmermann, quick!"

Rose Rita flew back upstairs. Lewis knelt beside his unconscious uncle, with only the flashlight to chase away the gloom and darkness of the cellar.

He was so worried about Uncle Jonathan that he even forgot to feel afraid of what might be lurking in the dark.

CHAPTER TWO

"Okay," rumbled Dr. Humphries in a deep voice like a bass viol, "how many fingers am I holding up?"

"Eleven," growled Jonathan Barnavelt, sitting propped on a big pile of pillows in his own bed. Lewis, standing at the foot of the bed, gulped hard. Had his uncle's accident made him lose his mind? But then he relaxed as Jonathan continued, "Of course, that's in binomial notation. In decimal terms, it's three. Does that satisfy you, you pill-pusher?"

Dr. Humphries laughed. "Well, your fall down the stairs didn't knock the orneriness out of you, anyhow! You take it easy for a couple of days, Jonathan, and call me if you have any unusual symptoms, like a bad headache, double vision, or tomato vines growing out of your ears!" He turned to Lewis, Rose Rita, and Mrs. Zimmermann.

"Nothing too much wrong with Bickering Barnavelt here. The scientific name for his ailment is bumpus nogginus, otherwise known as a crack on the head. He'll be fine."

"Thank you, Doctor," said Mrs. Zimmermann. "It was kind of you to come out so quickly."

The physician winked at her. "I charge more for a house call," he said cheerfully. "And besides, I love to drive fast. The cops don't dare stop me when I'm on an emergency call!" He picked up his leather case full of rattling square pill bottles, and wished them all a good afternoon.

As soon as the doctor was out of the door, Jonathan Barnavelt threw off the quilt that had covered him. He had come to in the cellar just as Mrs. Zimmermann and Rose Rita came running over, and he had made the climb to his bedroom under his own power. He hadn't undressed, and now he jammed his shoes onto his stockinged feet. "I feel like a prize nincompoop," he complained.

"What happened, Jonathan?" asked Mrs. Zimmermann.

Jonathan rubbed the top of his head gingerly. "Darned if I know. I heard someone on the cellar steps, or thought I did. So I opened the door and tried to turn on the light, but the bulb was on the fritz. Then I thought I heard Lewis call me. So I started down the stairs, and the next thing I remember is an almighty thump on the head and lots of pretty spinning colored stars. I guess I must have tripped in the dark." He tugged at his red beard. "Lewis, I suppose it wasn't you in the cellar, after all."

Lewis shook his head. "We were next door," he said. He explained how he and Rose Rita had hunted for Jonathan for several minutes before they found him.

"Odd," commented Jonathan. "I could have sworn I heard someone down there. Maybe we'd better check."

"Do you feel up to it?" asked Mrs. Zimmermann.

"I'm not a baby, Florence," replied Jonathan with a touch of exasperation. "I've had lots of bumps and thumps in my time, and none of them has killed me yet!"

Lewis's heart pounded. He hated to hear his uncle mention death. Ever since his own parents had died, Lewis had lived with a fear of being left alone in the world. He bit his lip, but didn't say anything.

Jonathan dug out a big flashlight, not the small one that was kept in the kitchen drawer, and they all trooped into the cellar. Jonathan fumbled on a shelf for a hundred-watt bulb. "Let me get this in, and we'll see if there's any sign of an intruder."

"Let Lewis do it," suggested Mrs. Zimmermann. "You have no business standing on a ladder after a head injury."

"Yes, Your Majesty," responded Jonathan. "Anything you wish. Lewis, drag out the stepladder."

Lewis climbed up on the ladder. The only light in the cellar hung from the ceiling in a conical green and white metal shade. He reached up to take out the old bulb and found it was loose. Surprised, he tightened it and almost fell off the ladder when it suddenly gave out a glaring white light.

"That's more like it," Jonathan said. "Lewis, what's wrong? You're white as a ghost."

"I—I didn't change the bulb," stammered Lewis. "S-someone must have loosened it on purpose!"

"Unlikely," his uncle said. "It probably just worked its way loose on its own. They sometimes do that, you know. It's caused when turning the light on and off alternately heats and cools the base, causing it to expand and contract—"

"Oh, expand and contract yourself, Brush Mush," said Mrs. Zimmermann tartly. "Cut out the Mr. Wizard stuff. Did you go over to the coal bin?"

"Not that I recall," Jonathan said thoughtfully. "I had just gotten to the bottom of the steps, when blooey! I fell flat on my kisser. Why?"

Mrs. Zimmermann pointed. "Because someone was down here, all right. Someone with big feet."

Lewis looked where she was pointing. The coal bin was empty and disused because Jonathan had changed the furnace over to oil years ago. But the big open bay still had a coating of grimy coal dust. Its back wall was a heavy sheet of plywood, covering a weird passageway that Jonathan had discovered shortly after Lewis had come to live there. Lewis saw what Mrs. Zimmermann had noticed: the faint coal-dust outline of shoe prints on the cellar floor, leading away from the coal bin.

"Strange," said Jonathan. He went to the bin and peered at the plywood. "Hmm. Someone has pulled this loose too." He tugged, and the plywood sheet fell away. Behind it was a plaster wall with a ragged opening leading into darkness. Jonathan shined his flashlight into the passage, which looked like a mine shaft. "Nothing was in here, so whoever it was must have gone away empty-handed and disappointed."

Mrs. Zimmermann stood beside him and touched his arm. "I don't like this at all. That is where Isaac Izard hid his Doomsday Clock."

Rose Rita gave Lewis a quick look. He had told her all about Izard, an evil magician who had owned the house before Jonathan. She knew that Izard and his equally wicked wife, Selenna, had plotted to end the world with a magical clock, and she knew that Lewis, Uncle Jonathan, and Mrs. Zimmermann had fought hard when Selenna Izard had risen from her tomb to complete the spell. "Was the clock still there?" she asked. "Could someone have been after it?"

"Not a chance," declared Jonathan firmly. "First, Lewis smashed the clock to smithereens, and Frizzy Wig and I disposed of the remains so that it could never be put together again. Second, no one knew that it had ever been here except for the Izards and us. We've never spread the word about it, and I know that Selenna Izard will never be able to rise from the dead and tromp around hunting the clock again. Besides, these footprints have to be size tens. Mrs. Izard was no beauty, but she didn't have feet the size of gunboats!"

"Th-then who broke in?" asked Lewis.

Jonathan shook his head, winced, and rubbed the lump on his head again. "Don't know, Lewis. Probably some tramp. Don't worry about it, though. I'm okay, and we'll carry on with our vacation plans."

"Aren't you going to tell the police?" demanded Rose Rita.

With a thoughtful expression, Jonathan said, "No, I don't think so. Nothing was taken, after all. And I'm not even sure that Mr. Intruder conked me on the bean. I still think I probably just tripped and took a header off the stair. It's my guess that whoever was down here has high-tailed it out of town. Just to be on the safe side, though, I think maybe Florence should cast some protective spells to keep Barnavelt Manor safe and sound while we're away. Feel up to it, O Enchantrix?"

Mrs. Zimmermann stuck out her tongue at Jonathan. "Pooh to you, Jonathan Barnavelt. Of course I feel up to it! I'll work up a honey of a spell that will zap any evil-intentioned intruder to kingdom come. You concentrate on getting over your cracked cranium, that's all!"

And for a time that seemed to end it. Jonathan and Lewis spent the next several days getting ready for their trip to the Upper Peninsula. Though Lewis remained jumpy, nothing happened. Sometimes he woke up in the night, thinking he heard furtive footsteps roaming the halls. But when he worked up the nerve to check, there was never anyone about.

Toward the end of June, they made the last few preparations. Jonathan had arranged for the part-time cleaning lady, Mrs. Holtz, to check on the house a couple of times a week and take in the newspapers. She also agreed to forward any important mail to the General Delivery window in Porcupine Bay. Then on a bright Friday morning everything was ready. Jonathan and Lewis had packed their clothes in the huge cardboard suitcase that had once belonged to Lewis's dad. They added a couple of fishing rods and reels, an assortment of books to read, and various other odds and ends.

Mrs. Zimmermann and Rose Rita were ready too. They were going to drive up, and Mrs. Zimmermann insisted that they make the trip in Bessie. She didn't trust Jonathan's car, which was an old 1935 Muggins Simoon, a boxy automobile like something out of an old-time movie. Luckily, the Plymouth Cranbrook had a roomy trunk. After some rearranging and muttering, Jonathan got everyone's bags and the fishing gear inside. Then they were off in a cloud of exhaust smoke, with Mrs. Zimmermann and Jonathan in the front seat and Lewis and Rose Rita in the back.

It was a long trip, up through Lansing, the state capital of Michigan, and then through small towns like Ithaca, Mount Pleasant, and Rosebush. In Houghton Lake they switched drivers, and Jonathan promptly got them lost on a shortcut. Mrs. Zimmermann kidded him about that, but when he stopped at a diner to ask directions, the place smelled so good that they decided to eat there. The hamburgers were the most delicious ones that Lewis had ever tasted, and with a beaming smile, Jonathan pointed out that even if they were off the track, his food-finding instincts were working perfectly.

They got back onto the main highway soon afterward, and as they rolled along through the summer afternoon, they sang crazy songs: "The Hut-Sut Song," "Mairzy

Doats," and "Flat-Foot Floogie." They all joined in on that tune's nonsensical refrain, "Floy-doy, floy-doy, floy-doy!" Late that day they stopped at a motor hotel, a group of little cabins scattered beneath pines. Mrs. Zimmermann and Rose Rita took one cabin, and Jonathan and Lewis took the one next door. That night Lewis got the first really good night's sleep he had had in weeks, despite his uncle's world-class snoring.

The next morning, they drove onto a ferryboat for the ride across to the Upper Peninsula. Then they turned west. Jonathan mentioned that the Michigan citizens who lived on the Upper Peninsula thought that people from the southern part of the state were a little nuts, "and vicy-versy."

"Michiganders," corrected Mrs. Zimmermann.

Jonathan snorted. "I hate that word! Anyway, it would only apply to the men. The women would have to be Michigeese!"

They squabbled good-naturedly like that through the whole morning. Occasionally the road took them within sight of Lake Superior, which to Lewis looked as big as an ocean. Sometimes sailing boats would be here and there on the rolling water, leaning against the wind as they skimmed along. Other times the lake just looked vast and empty, slate-gray under an increasingly cloudy sky.

It was afternoon by the time they reached the town of Porcupine Bay. It turned out to be a half circle of buildings and houses clinging to the edge of the water. Rose Rita had directions from her grandfather to meet him in the general store facing the long wharf. They found the place, Mrs. Zimmermann parked Bessie, and they all piled out of the Plymouth, stretching their cramped legs.

The store was cavernous and dark, and it smelled of cheese and fish. Some old men were playing checkers at three little tables in front of the counter, and a very short man, no more than five feet tall, stood at the cash register paying for two bags of groceries. Jonathan waited until the customer had picked up his bags and then spoke to the man at the cash register: "Hi. We're supposed to meet Albert Galway here."

The counterman had rusty-brown hair about the texture of a Brillo pad. He nodded and said, "Yep, he'll be in before long. He told me he was expecting you. You're Mr. Jonathan Barnavelt, I s'pose?"

Lewis heard a sudden crash. He looked behind him. The short man had dropped one of his grocery bags. Cans of salmon, pork and beans, and peas rumbled across the rough wood floor. One of the cans bumped against Lewis's foot, and he bent to pick it up.

The stranger's face jerked into a ghastly smile. "Th-thank you," he said in a hoarse voice. He reached out a bony hand to retrieve the can of salmon that Lewis offered him. Lewis saw that his fingers were dirty, deeply grained with black oil, and that all his fingernails had black grime under them. For some reason Lewis shivered. The little man had an ugly face, with one thick eyebrow that went all the way across. His nose was round and upturned, almost like a pig's snout. And his teeth were yellow and snaggly. But he seemed reasonably grateful as he repacked his bag and hurried out, letting the screen door slam behind him.

"You get some pretty strange customers in here, Jake," one of the checker players said. "I hope you made sure the money that character gave you isn't counterfeit. I wouldn't trust that Clusko guy any farther'n I could heave him."

"Clusko's okay," the counterman replied. "He comes in, buys what he wants, and pays up. He don't hang around playing checkers and tellin' lies like some people I know!"

The other checker players laughed at that, and even the man who had objected to Clusko's presence chuckled.

Not long after that the screen door opened and Lewis saw Albert Galway step into the store. Though he was in his eighties, he stood straight as a ramrod. He wore a jaunty white yachting cap perched atop his bald head, a dark blue double-breasted blazer over a white shirt with no tie, white trousers, and white shoes. "Hi, Rose Rita," he said as soon as he had stepped in. "Sorry about the delay, folks. I was making sure that some fuel oil would be delivered to the house. Even in June it gets kind of chilly out on the lake!"

They all climbed back into Bessie, and Mr. Galway directed Mrs. Zimmermann to a pier where a blue and white sailboat was moored. Lewis couldn't wait to climb aboard her. He and Rose Rita helped lug the suitcases over, and then Mrs. Zimmermann parked Bessie in a secure lot near the pier. Grampa Galway helped Mrs. Zimmermann, Rose Rita, and Lewis climb onto the vessel.

Jonathan saluted the quarterdeck—really the tiller—and said, "Permission to come aboard?"

Grampa Galway laughed. "Granted," he said, and Jonathan joined the rest. "Welcome to the good ship *Sunfish*. And now if Lewis will cast off the bowline and Rose Rita will help me run up the sail, we'll go out to Ivarhaven Island!"

It was a grand trip, though the gray sky looked increasingly stormy. With its white triangular sail billowing, the *Sunfish* skimmed over the dark water. The wind was fresh and steady, and Lewis thought this vacation might turn out to be a lot of fun after all.

He was mistaken about that. Very badly mistaken, as it turned out.

CHAPTER THREE

For four days and nights Lewis enjoyed himself immensely. They were staying in a house that belonged to a Mr. Marvin. "Jim Marvin," explained Grampa Galway. "He was a shavetail lieutenant in the old *Hull* back in 1917. I was older'n him, but of course I was just an ordinary seaman first class. Well, in the middle of the Atlantic one night, a German U-boat attacked us. Sent a torpedo amidships. It was a heck of an explosion, and I saw Lieutenant Marvin fall right over the rail. Everyone was runnin' this way and that, yellin' at the top of their lungs. You know the old 'General Order for Emergencies,' Lewis?"

Lewis shook his head, a smile of anticipation on his face.

With great relish Grampa Galway recited, "'When in danger or in doubt, run in circles, scream and shout!'

Well, sir, that's what the crew seemed to be doing. I grabbed a life ring and did a swan dive into the Atlantic. Talk about cold! Anyway, I spotted Lieutenant Marvin splashing and floundering in the light of the fire—the *Hull* was ablaze by then—and got to him with the life ring. By then the gunners had finally shaken themselves awake, and they started pounding the U-boat. Finally sank her too, and by then someone on deck had seen us by the light of the flares and picked us up. Luckily, they put out the fire and we limped into port. Well, ever since then, Jim Marvin's been a friend of mine."

Jim Marvin had made a lot of money in oil and steel after World War I, and he had bought an entire island, Ivarhaven, to build his dream house on. It was a shining white modernistic mansion, terraced and stacked in layers on the side of a hill. It had glass walls everywhere to give fantastic views of the lake. At the flattened-off top of the hill were a tennis court, a croquet court, and a tall flagpole. Every clear morning at dawn, Lewis and Rose Rita trooped there to run up the American flag, and every evening at sunset they brought it down and folded it.

Wednesday, the fifth day of their visit, began with a thin, cool rain. Despite the weather Grampa Galway said he was going to run over to Porcupine Bay, five miles away, in the sailboat. Lewis volunteered to go with him. He donned a yellow slicker and did such a good job of handling the sail that Grampa Galway pronounced him an able-bodied sailor as they tied up at the pier. Lewis swelled with pride.

They visited the general store, where Mr. Galway bought bread, milk, and some other supplies. Lewis noticed that the old checker players weren't around. Too rainy for them to come to the store, he supposed. In fact, except for a tall man with steel-gray hair who was also shopping, he and Grampa Galway had the store pretty much to themselves. They hauled their purchases to the counter. The clerk rang them up, then said, "Oh, yeah, I almost forgot. Some mail for you." He rummaged around under the counter and came up with a handful of letters. "For Mr. Barnavelt," he said, handing them over.

Lewis took them. He and Grampa Galway started out, each carrying two brown paper bags of groceries. They stood for a moment on the porch of the little store, looking at the steady rain. Suddenly the door behind them opened, and the gray-haired man said, "There's one more letter. May I give it to you?" He waved a manila envelope. It was about nine by twelve inches.

"Uh, sure," said Lewis, shifting his bags so he could take it from him. "Thanks."

"You're entirely welcome." The stranger smiled. He was taller than Grampa Galway and pretty thin. He wore dark trousers and a dark blue windbreaker, and his face looked weather-beaten. "Glad to have had the opportunity." He went back inside the store.

Lewis looked at the envelope curiously. In the corner someone had pasted half a dozen three-cent stamps. They were pale blue, and they pictured a long iron ore freighter ship, with a map of the five Great Lakes over it. "Soo

Locks, Sault Sainte Marie," the stamps read at the top, and at the bottom: "A Century of Great Lakes Transportation." Lewis had never seen these stamps before.

He glanced at the address. In spiky handwriting, someone had directed the envelope to "Lewis Barnavelt, General Delivery, Porcupine Bay, Mich." Who would be writing him? Not his English pen pal, Bertie Woodring, who didn't even know he was up here. Anyway, the handwriting was unfamiliar.

He had no time to find out, because Grampa Galway was ready to go. Lewis stuffed the envelope down into one of the grocery bags to keep it dry, and the two hurried off the porch and ran down to the pier. The rain was worse, gray curtains of it lashing across the lake. They stowed the groceries in the boat's cabin, cast off, and fought their way toward Ivarhaven Island. "Hang on, Lewis," bellowed Grampa Galway. "These blows can get kind of rough!"

It was almost like riding a roller coaster. The wind got up to a stiff gale, and they had to shorten the sail. Lewis held the tiller, steering the boat, while Grampa Galway hauled the sail partway down and then tied off the bottom part, securing it to the boom. "Keep us from blowing over on our beam ends," he said when he came back. "Now, if my dead reckoning isn't too far out, we should be seeing the island about any time now."

Lewis felt a little queasy, but suddenly the green bulk of Ivarhaven materialized out of the rain ahead. They brought the *Sunfish* into her slip, moored her bow and stern, and dropped the sail. Then they hurried into the mansion with their four dripping bags of groceries.

"How was it?" asked Rose Rita as they squelched into the kitchen.

Grampa Galway shook his head. "Not a fit day out for man nor beast. We probably should've waited, but we were all out of milk!"

They unpacked the groceries and Lewis pulled out his envelope. "Somebody sent me a letter," he told Rose Rita as the two of them walked into the study.

"Who?" she asked.

"Let's find out," returned Lewis. He plopped the envelope down on the desk and sat in the rolling chair. Then he peeled the flap of the envelope open. It was pretty damp, and the glue gave way easily. He reached inside and pulled out something. But it wasn't a letter.

It was a single folded page torn from some old book. A big book too, because when he unfolded it, the page was about ten inches wide and twelve inches long. Lewis flattened it on the study table and blinked in amazement at what he saw.

One side of the page was thickly printed with a Latin text in Gothic lettering. The other side was taken up by a steel engraving, a scene rendered in densely cross-hatched lines of ink. On the right, a king sat on an ornate throne, a stern expression on his bearded face. His outstretched hand held a scepter. On the left side of the picture stood four soldiers. Between them cowered a mysterious figure in a hood and cape. You couldn't tell whether it was a man or a woman. At the bottom of the engraving, in fancy lettering, was the title of the picture:

Contradicto Salomonis cum demonio nocturno.

"What in the world . . . ?" asked Rose Rita.

"I don't know," admitted Lewis. "But the Latin means 'Solomon's Debate with a Demon of the Night.'" Then he noticed something that made him feel cold and brought goose bumps popping out on his arms. In the lower right corner of the illustration, the throne of King Solomon cast a deep black shadow. Only as he stared at it, Lewis realized it wasn't a shadow at all, but some kind of *creature*. It hunkered beside the throne, its spidery limbs hugging itself. Its body seemed to be covered with matted, shaggy black hair. Just visible at its left shoulder was its right hand, nearly skeletal. Like Solomon, it was pointing its finger toward the cowled figure as if in accusation. But worst of all were the eyes, round saucers that seemed to glow at the viewer with an inner hatred.

Lewis felt his stomach lurch. He had the uncanny certainty that the artist had not made up this monstrosity. It had been drawn from a living model.

"What's wrong?" demanded Rose Rita. "Hey, Lewis, what do you see?"

"L-look at this *thing*," said Lewis. He put a shaking finger on the freakish image.

Rose Rita frowned. "There's nothing to get upset about, Lewis. That's just the shadow of the throne."

"No," insisted Lewis. "See? Here's its head, and here are its eyes—"

Rose Rita took the paper from him. "I don't think so. Those two white blobs aren't eyes, they're ornaments on the throne. See, here are two more. It's just a shadow."

Lewis forced himself to look more closely. Oddly, when he concentrated on making out the hideous creature, it seemed to fade away. Now the picture looked as if Rose Rita were right. It was just a dark pool of shadow with some jagged edges. Still, Lewis found it hard to breathe. He knew that he was going to dream about that thing.

The Latin text on the other side of the page didn't help at all. It was a sort of list giving examples of evil acts of witchcraft:

III. *Animals sicken and die, their maladies caused by magic.*
IV. *The evil eye brings misfortune.*
 V. *Deep secrets are known by the sorcerer, though no one speaks of them.*

Lewis translated that much for Rose Rita. The list went on like that. "It doesn't say anything about Solomon at all," finished Lewis.

Rose Rita just shrugged. "I guess the picture may be King Solomon delivering judgment on the Witch of Endor or something. Crazy thing to send you. Is there a note?"

Lewis shook the envelope. "No. I don't think—" He broke off as a slip of paper fluttered from the envelope. It twirled through the air, and he made a grab for it, catching it before it hit the floor.

"So what is it?" asked Rose Rita, craning to see. "Some kind of weird advertisement or something?"

Lewis's hands were shaking. The slip was parchment, not paper, and it felt odd in his fingers, as if it were writhing with some life of its own. Marching across the slip in three rows were some very strange angular letters. They had been drawn in rusty-red ink, and they made no sense at all to Lewis. "Some kind of foreign language," he told Rose Rita.

She looked at the writing. "No," she said slowly. "I don't think so. These are runes. I can't read them all, but this one is a *T*, and I think this one's an *E*."

Lewis knew that runes were a kind of alphabet used by the ancient Norse and Germanic peoples to leave inscriptions carved in stones. Because of that, they were angular and odd-looking. But beyond that, he had no idea what the inscription might mean. He certainly couldn't read a fifteen-hundred-year-old alphabet!

"Maybe we'd better show this to Mrs. Zimmermann," he said.

"Good idea," agreed Rose Rita.

They found her right back where they had begun, in the kitchen. She was happily preparing lunch for everyone: homemade vegetable-noodle soup, thick chicken sandwiches on sourdough bread, and a blueberry pie for dessert. But she stopped her work the moment she saw the distressed expression on Lewis's face.

Lewis and Rose Rita quickly explained what had happened. Mrs. Zimmermann studied the book illustration for a long time, but then she shook her head. "I'm sorry,

Lewis, but I can't make out your monster. I think Rose Rita is right—it's just an optical illusion caused by the light and shadow. However, let me take a look at the parchment. Hmm."

Mrs. Zimmermann scowled down at the rust-red runes scratched on the slip of parchment. Then she pushed her spectacles up into her wild nest of white hair and peered very closely at the lettering. "This is strange, indeed," she muttered. "Well, these are not *futhark* runes, which are the standard type used by the Vikings and the Norsemen. They're Celtic. I think they're Manx runes, which originated on the Isle of Man, near Great Britain. I can't read them all, but I can just about make out this part: *You are granted forty-eight.* To me that's about as clear as a bowl of pea soup. Does it make any sense to you?"

"No. Forty-eight what?" Lewis asked.

"That I don't know," answered Mrs. Zimmermann in a thoughtful voice. "Forty-eight coconut cream pies? Forty-eight free issues of *Boy's Life* magazine? A tour of the forty-eight states? I have no idea! As soon as we get back to New Zebedee, though, I'll consult some textbooks on runes and ancient languages. Maybe with luck I can decipher the rest."

Lewis took a deep breath. "Don't tell Uncle Jonathan about this, okay?"

Mrs. Zimmermann popped her spectacles back into place. She stared at him with wide eyes. "Why not?"

With a miserable shrug, Lewis said, "Well, he's been happy the last few days, fishing and sailing. And we're gonna be here for another three days. After all that business with the bump on his head, I'd like for him to have a good vacation and not worry."

Mrs. Zimmermann smiled and tapped her chin with her finger. "Very well, Lewis. But I'll tell you what I do plan to do. I am going to make some telephone calls to some friends of mine who know about secret languages and mystical signs. If there's something witchy about this piece of parchment, they'll be sure to know. Meanwhile, keep it safe. I'd suggest putting it your wallet and treating it like a thousand-dollar bill. And try not to worry."

"Okay," said Lewis.

With a kindly smile, Mrs. Zimmermann patted his hand. "I know that's easy advice to give and hard advice to take! But Rose Rita and I will help you solve this mystery if we can. Until we have something to go on, sit tight and don't give in to worry and woe. All right, Lewis?"

"All right," Lewis told her. But that was much easier said than done.

CHAPTER FOUR

Mrs. Zimmermann was as good as her word. She never mentioned the odd parchment to Jonathan. Still, Lewis found that his vacation was ruined. At night when he was trying to go to sleep, a vision of the horrible, shaggy, emaciated monster floated just behind his eyelids.

He sat up in bed one evening trying to read a mystery novel. As usual he was munching something as he read. In this case it was a package of chocolate-covered peanuts. Lewis should have been comfortable. He had three big puffy pillows behind him. The novel was about a peculiar murder in which all the victim's clothes were turned backward. But Lewis found it very hard to concentrate.

He lost the thread of the story and turned back a page to reread it. Staring at the book, he popped a chocolate-covered peanut into his mouth. But when he bit into it, something was terribly wrong.

It wasn't crunchy, but squishy. And it *moved* in his mouth!

Lewis sputtered and spat. The candy plopped onto the bed—and then it sprouted legs! It scuttled over the edge of the bed.

Lewis's stomach lurched. He looked down at the box in his left hand. Roaches were streaming out of it, dozens of them. Their oily brown wings glistened in the light from his bedside lamp. They were scrambling up his arms, heading for his face!

Gagging and choking, Lewis jumped out of bed—

The book crashed to the floor. The candy box fell beside it, and two or three chocolate-covered peanuts rolled out. Lewis stood with his back to the wall, frantically slapping at himself.

The insects had vanished. Lewis blinked. It had been a dream, he realized. He had dozed off while reading the book and had dreamed the disgusting stream of roaches. He stumbled to the bathroom and brushed his teeth extra hard. Then he rinsed his mouth with cold water four times. Only then did he return to his bedroom and pick up the book and the box of candy. Lewis dumped the box into the trash. He didn't think he'd ever want chocolate-covered peanuts again.

After that, though, Lewis didn't even try to read when he went to bed at night. He could no more concentrate on a book than he could go for a stroll across the deep waters of Lake Superior.

He found it all doubly painful because he didn't want to ruin everyone else's vacation. In ordinary times he would have loved the whole trip. The house was fascinating, with balconies overlooking the lake, and a whole library of its own. True, the books were not something Lewis would read, volumes like *A Mineralogical Field Guide to the Upper Midwest* and *Topographic Indicators of Oil-Bearing Strata*, but they gave the room a cozy feel that any bookworm would welcome. And there was much to do besides reading.

Jonathan loved to fish off the dock, and he caught some beauties: lake trout, steelhead, and coho. Lewis and Rose Rita joined him sometimes, though Lewis was squeamish about taking the fish off the hooks. They threw most of their catch back, but on one evening they had a big fish fry, with Jonathan smacking his lips over the tasty trout that he had caught himself.

After the stormy trip into Porcupine Bay, Lewis didn't go back aboard the *Sunfish*. Rose Rita and Grampa Galway went in on Friday and returned with some more mail. Nothing came for Lewis, to his relief, but Jonathan got the forwarded electric bill and a letter from his sister in Osee Five Hills. All in all Lewis should have enjoyed the break from routine, if only he could have gotten his mind off the vaguely threatening piece of parchment and the much more frightening steel engraving.

Their week on Ivarhaven Island drew to a close. They planned to drive back to New Zebedee on Sunday. At Mrs. Zimmermann's suggestion, they all agreed to go on a boating expedition on the last Saturday of their stay.

"We'll pack a picnic lunch," said Mrs. Zimmermann cheerfully. "I'll make my special potato salad and fry a big batch of chicken. We'll have chocolate cake, fresh rolls, lemonade, and a great big thermos of iced tea. Then we'll find a particularly interesting island to land on. Maybe even an unexplored one!"

"One where the hand of man has never set foot," put in Jonathan with a mischievous wink. "And we can claim it in the name of truth, justice, and the American way!"

"Oh, that shouldn't be much of a problem. Around here there are islands aplenty," said Grampa Galway, rubbing his hands together. "And the weather report for Saturday sounds just right. We can do some real sailing! Hoist up the sails and see how much speed we can get out of our trusty vessel!"

And so it was all arranged. Saturday dawned beautifully bright and clear, with a steady wind from the northwest. Everyone was cheerful as they loaded up the boat—everyone, that is, except Lewis. He had to force himself to appear to enjoy the trip.

By nine o'clock the *Sunfish* leaned into the dark waters, cutting a frothy white wake as she skimmed along. Rose Rita and Lewis took turns at the tiller as they sped across the calm water. Grampa Galway showed them how to tack, how to bring the boat about, and how to wear ship. Those were different ways of turning into or away from the wind, and ordinarily Lewis would have felt like a dashing naval hero or pirate king. Because of his worries and his lack of sleep, though, he just felt light-headed and groggy.

They began looking for a picnic island about eleven o'clock. Some small rocks loomed up to the right, but everyone agreed they appeared too damp and uncomfortable. One pine-covered island looked likely until they approached it and saw it was thickly posted with stern "No Trespassing" signs. They left that one behind. Suddenly Uncle Jonathan said, "Look over there, to port."

Lewis had to smile at that. His uncle had taken to boating the way a duckling takes to water. He was always coming up with words like "abaft" and "amidships." Holding on to the tiller, Lewis leaned so that he could see under the boom and looked off to the left, the direction that sailors and his uncle Jonathan referred to as "port."

He wasn't sure what he saw. It was a shimmering in the air, like heat waves dancing off a hot asphalt road. The effect was bizarre. It looked as if a big part of the lake were wriggling like blue-gray Jell-O, rising up into the air for a few feet, and then dissolving like smoke blowing away on a breeze. "What *is* that?" asked Lewis.

Grampa Galway shaded his eyes with his hand. He shook his head doubtfully. "Strangest thing I've seen in these waters. Looks mighty like a Sahara mirage. Except the Sahara is about fifty million times drier than Lake Superior, and considerably hotter! Bear to port, Lewis. Let's check it out."

Lewis gave Rose Rita a sick, pleading look. She seemed to understand that he was unusually anxious. "Want me to take the tiller?" she asked.

He shook his head. Maybe it was silly, but he hated looking like a chicken in front of Rose Rita and his friends. He moved the tiller until the bow of the *Sunfish* pointed directly at the strange phenomenon.

"It isn't a waterspout," mused Mrs. Zimmermann, clapping one hand to the crown of her purple sun hat to keep it from blowing right off her head. "And it can't be gasoline fumes or reflections of the sun."

Jonathan held to a line and leaned far out. "It isn't fog or mist either. Very peculiar! Maybe we've discovered a submarine volcano or a completely unknown atmospheric condition."

The *Sunfish* drew nearer and nearer to the shimmering curtain of air. Lewis tightened his grip on the tiller. Part of him wanted to yank it desperately, to turn away from whatever lay ahead, to flee. But what would everyone think of him? No one else was panicky. He had to force himself to be calm. Taking a deep breath, Lewis held his course.

Seconds before the bow of the sailboat could penetrate the glimmering, wavering barrier, it vanished, and suddenly ahead of them was a green island. Lewis blinked. They were only a couple of hundred yards away, and it was as if the island had just materialized out of thin air.

It was a domed islet, perhaps ten or twelve acres in area. To Lewis it appeared to be a hill that rose abruptly out of the water. Its fringes were heavily wooded with blue-green fir trees, but these stopped halfway up the hillside. The rounded summit looked grassy and smooth. Strangest of all, rising straight up from the shoulder of the hill was a stark black column. At first Lewis thought it was the trunk of a tall, dead tree. Then, as they drew closer, he realized it was a man-made structure of some sort. A dark tower, rising maybe a hundred feet into the air from its base.

"This is peculiar," grunted Grampa Galway.

"Why?" asked Rose Rita.

Her grandfather lifted his yachting cap and scratched his bald head. "Because no island should be here at all. I've sailed this way before, and I know this place is not marked on the chart! But we were hoping to make a discovery, so I say we find an anchorage."

The others agreed, and Lewis lacked the heart to be the only one who objected. Grampa Galway took the tiller from Lewis, and Lewis went forward. He stood in the bow and stared as the sailboat turned and started around the southwestern shore of the little island. The sight of it filled him with a strange sense of dread. He clenched his hands and hoped that they wouldn't be able to find an anchorage. For some reason he didn't want to set foot on the place.

For a short while that looked like a pretty good bet. The steep, brushy sides of the island rose from the water, with no inlet or sheltered spot for the boat to anchor. But then, on the southernmost side of the island, Lewis saw a creek tumbling down a rocky bed. It spilled over smooth brown stones like scattered potatoes and foamed into Lake Superior, making a little inlet. Just within the inlet stood a solid-looking wood pier.

"We'll tie up there," announced Grampa Galway. "Jonathan, get the sounding pole and make sure we've got enough water. No sense in running aground!"

Jonathan stood in the bow with a long pole. He thrust this straight down in the water, testing the depth. "No bottom so far," he stated as Rose Rita shortened sail. The *Sunfish* slowed until it was barely drifting, and Grampa Galway steered her toward the pier with expert attention. Just before the bow bumped the pier, Jonathan said, "We've got a good eight feet of water. Safe enough!"

Then the boat very gently nudged up to the pier. Rose Rita and Uncle Jonathan jumped out and helped with the mooring lines, and a very unwilling Lewis finally climbed from the *Sunfish*. He was carrying the picnic basket. "Maybe this isn't such a hot idea," he mumbled. "Maybe this whole island belongs to somebody who wouldn't like us tying up here."

Rose Rita shook her head. "Then why didn't Mr. Whosis, the Master of Mystery Island, plant some 'No Trespassing' signs like the ones we saw earlier? This might be a state park or something, for all we know. Anyway, there's no other boat here, and it's first come, first served as far as I'm concerned."

"This is a curious place," said Jonathan. "That's for sure. But it seems solid and harmless enough. I don't know what the shimmery-glimmery was that hid it, but maybe it was just some trick of the sun and mist over the water. Anyway, we're here now."

From the pier a crooked, grassy path zigged and zagged this way and that through the dark firs, climbing the hillside. They followed it into a sudden grassy clearing. There they found a stone cottage, a little one-story house no more than twenty feet square. The steep roof was shingled with flat charcoal-colored slates. The cottage had only one door and a single shuttered window. No smoke rose from its stone chimney, and the place looked deserted and as lifeless as a skull.

Lewis wiped his face. He was sweating, and not just from the effort of carrying their picnic lunch and climbing up the trail. He could not shake off a strange feeling of dread. Yet the island seemed completely normal. Grasshoppers zinged in the grass, and cardinals and jays chattered in the trees. Even so, their surroundings gave Lewis a case of the heebie-jeebies. He kept expecting something terrible to jump out at them any second. But everything looked very serene.

"I'd say nobody's home," observed Mrs. Zimmermann as they walked toward the cottage. For a moment they stood in front of the closed door. Nothing inside the house stirred. "Of course, whoever lives here must have to get back and forth by boat, and we didn't see any boat, so they must be out. Well, we'll be extra-special neat when we have our picnic. I don't think we'll trouble anyone. Come on. Let's climb the hill and see what we can see, like the bear that went over the mountain."

The trail continued through the trees on the other side of the clearing. Lewis began to tire of lugging the picnic hamper. Then, just as he was about to ask if he could set it down and rest for a moment, the group came out onto a second clearing, much stranger than the first.

Before them reared the dark tower. It was made of curved blocks of some black stone shot through with tiny cobwebby streaks of gray. Lewis tilted his head back. The structure might have been a skinny lighthouse, except it looked like no lighthouse he had ever seen. For one thing, it did not seem to have a door, at least not at ground level.

But leading up to the very top of the tower on one side was a precarious-looking set of steps, very narrow, and rising like a flying buttress supporting a cathedral wall. He had not seen them from the water. Probably the angle had been wrong and the tower itself had hidden them. Just looking at the steep steps made Lewis feel dizzy. They had no handrails, and each step was barely a foot wide. Only a fool or a very desperate person would attempt such a climb, he thought. One slip, and you'd break your neck.

"Hmm," said Mrs. Zimmermann, touching her chin thoughtfully. "Curiouser and curiouser, as Lewis Carroll wrote. This is a very steep lawn! And I wonder what on earth the tower is supposed to commemorate."

Slanting upward to the north from the base of the tower was the lawn Mrs. Zimmermann had mentioned. Someone obviously took good care of it. The grass was trimmed short, with no weeds sprouting anywhere, and curving walkways of crushed white gravel crisscrossed the space. Scattered about on the lawn were groups of grotesque metal sculptures. On the west side was a spray of six iron poles, each about ten feet long. They leaned from a round stone base like gigantic jonquils placed in a vase too large for them. At the end of each pole was the wrought-iron figure of a flying bat. A few steps away stood a circle of seven five-foot tall stone pillars, each one fluted like a Corinthian column. On the top of every column was a gleaming life-sized human skull made of transparent quartz crystal. Past that was a tiny graveyard, walled in by a black wrought-iron fence. Eight white marble tombstones marked the graves, but they were blank and smooth, with no names chiseled on them. Beyond were more groups of odd sculptures: five jagged lightning bolts, a standing human figure with upraised arms, three staring glass eyeballs, six things that looked like gallows complete with dangling nooses, and more. Lewis counted a dozen different clusters of sculpture in all.

"I don't like this place," pronounced Mrs. Zimmermann firmly, hugging herself as if the day had turned cold. "Someone went to a lot of expense and trouble to put all these geegaws up, and from the looks of them, I'd say that the builder was constructing a park for the mentally deranged."

Jonathan stood beside her, staring at the graves. He nodded. "I agree with you, Florence. This is no place for a picnic, anyway. Let's get away from here."

The group hurried back down the path faster than they had climbed. Rose Rita grabbed the handle of the picnic hamper and helped Lewis carry it. "Thanks," he grunted, grateful for her aid.

They passed the closed-up cottage and then clambered down toward the pier. The *Sunfish* waited for them there, and everyone except Lewis climbed aboard. He stayed on the pier to cast off the bowline. Just before he stepped onto the deck, he turned for a last look at the island.

The grassy path twisted and turned into the shadows of the firs. The shade looked unnaturally deep, as if it were evening, not noon. Somehow the woods were a little too dark, a little too murky. Then Lewis saw something that almost made him shriek.

One length of the grassy path lay in sunlight, except for a wavering patch of shadow. As Lewis stared so hard that he felt his eyes were about to bug out of his head, the shadowy patch moved. It shot out something that could have been a long, skinny, crooked arm. At the end of it a skeletal hand seemed to clutch the grass. The dark patch crept forward.

And then it opened two yellow eyes and glared at him.

Lewis jumped onto the *Sunfish*. "Let's get out of here!" he screeched, his voice rising to a high pitch.

Grampa Galway had cast off the stern line, and Jonathan was leaning on his sounding pole, pushing the bow away from the pier. Rose Rita pulled the line that raised the sail, and with a whump! it filled with air and pulled the boat away from shore.

Lewis looked back. The dark patch was still there. Only now it was clearly nothing more than the shadow of a tree branch falling across the sunny spot.

Had he seen what he thought he had seen? For one terrifying moment, he had been sure that the monster from "Solomon's Debate" had found him. It had crept down the pathway, crawling like an inky cat slinking low to the ground with prey in sight. And it had fixed him with pale yellow eyes filled with hatred.

Lewis stared at the shadow as the *Sunfish* left the island. It shrank with distance. Then suddenly, the island simply winked out of existence. It was gone as if it had never existed. Lewis could not even see the ghostly, shimmery waves that had marked it before.

"Where did it go?" asked Rose Rita, standing beside him.

Everyone looked back. Grampa Galway cleared his throat. "Guess we're making better time than I thought," he said, his voice sounding shaky. "Must be going fifteen knots."

"Sure," agreed Jonathan. "Well, good riddance, I say! We'll find some more pleasant place to stuff our faces with Florence's fried chicken and potato salad than that playground for madmen."

Lewis knew his uncle very well. He caught the notes of doubt and uncertainty in Jonathan's voice. And somehow he sensed that their troubles were only beginning.

CHAPTER FIVE

On the first night home from the trip, Lewis slept much better than he had in days. By Monday morning he was beginning to think that maybe the worst was over. Mrs. Zimmermann came over to fix breakfast, as she often did. She hated eating alone, and she knew very well that Jonathan Barnavelt could hardly boil water, let alone make a delicious breakfast of hash browns, scrambled eggs with cheese, and tasty sausage. The three of them enjoyed the meal, and Mrs. Zimmermann seemed extra kind as she talked to Lewis. He knew she would research the strange picture and the parchment covered in ancient runes. If something was truly wrong, she would find a way to put it right.

For the first time in a long time, Lewis decided not to

worry. He had read none of the books he had planned to read on vacation. He selected one of them, a detective story by a writer named Ellery Queen, and settled down under the chestnut tree in the front yard to read it. It was a real puzzler, and it occupied him for most of the day.

Rose Rita came over after dinner that evening. Lewis and Jonathan were in the front parlor watching a western on TV when she arrived. "Hi," she said. "I thought I'd go and see the Fourth of July fireworks at the athletic field. Want to come?"

Uncle Jonathan smiled wearily. "I'm pooped after our vacation and driving halfway back home. But you and Lewis go if you want. Grab a couple of sparklers for Florence and me!"

Lewis didn't much feel like seeing the show, but Rose Rita obviously wanted company. He mumbled, "Sure, I'll go with you. Want to ride our bikes over?"

Rose Rita pulled a long face. "No can do. I banged over the curb just before we left and warped my front wheel. Dad still hasn't gotten around to fixing it."

Lewis shrugged. "Doesn't matter. We can walk."

Usually Lewis liked walking the streets of his hometown. New Zebedee was stuffed with interesting old houses. Some were like Victorian layer cakes with so much decoration that the houses seemed more like excuses for pilasters and fancy cornices and gingerbread than places for living. Others were built in different styles, from elegant stone Georgian to wood and plaster Tudor. One was even an imitation of a South Seas mansion. It had been built back in the 1800's by a New Zebedee native who had been a representative of the United States to the Sandwich Islands.

On that Monday evening, though, Lewis hardly noticed his surroundings. He was beginning to feel a little jumpy again, but he didn't know why. Rose Rita respected his silence. They spoke very little as they joined a crowd that was strolling over to the athletic field on the edge of town. People covered the bleachers already, and the newcomers spread out blankets and towels on the grass. The town's brass band was tootling away, led by the mayor, Mr. Hugo Davis. Lewis had to grin at the sight of the portly Mr. Davis stuffed into his red and white bandleader's costume. His collar was so tight that his eyes were bugging out, and his scarlet face contrasted with his snowy white hair. But he was waving his baton with enthusiasm, directing the band as they played "The Stars and Stripes Forever."

Lewis and Rose Rita spoke to a few kids they knew from school. On the far side of the field Lewis recognized Tarby Corrigan, one of New Zebedee's top athletes. Tarby and Lewis once had struck up a friendship, but that had ended when Tarby began to tease Lewis about being fat. As Rose Rita and Lewis looked around for a place to sit, Lewis noticed Tarby looking at them. He didn't wave, and Lewis knew that Tarby was pretending he did not exist, as usual.

Rose Rita said, "I don't want to go down onto the field. Let's look over here." They found a grassy spot on the hillside where they would have a good view, and listened as the band played and the sky grew darker. Finally, mopping his face with a red bandanna, Mr. Davis held up his hands and said, "And now the high point of the evening. Let the fireworks begin!"

Far across the athletic field, in a roped-off area, the shadowy forms of five men hustled about. One of them stooped down, a glowing red stick in his hand. He touched a fuse, and with a whizz, a rocket shot up into the air, trailing a skirt of golden sparks. It whistled as it rose, then exploded into a sphere of brilliant yellow stars. A moment later the *boom!* rolled into the crowd as everyone said, "Ooh!"

More rockets and fireworks followed. Some were vivid green, some blue, some dazzling white, some red. Some were fired into the air from stubby mortars. Others zipped up under their own power, leaving straight or wavy trails of light. Catherine wheels spun and fizzed, and Roman candles shot globes of fire high into the air. At the big finish dozens of rockets went up at once, making Lewis's ears throb with their bangs and blasts. The explosions dazzled him, and he joined in the applause at the end. Then everyone got up and started to drift out of the athletic field, all talking at once about what a good show it had been.

Lewis and Rose Rita walked downtown with a crowd of other people, past the Farmers Seed and Feed on the corner of Main and Eagle. They crossed Main Street near the drugstore and walked toward the Pottinger house on Mansion Street. Suddenly they were alone. "I liked the starburst ones best," said Rose Rita, continuing a discussion they had begun in front of Heemsoth's Rexall Drug Store. "I'll bet they were the kind of rocket that Francis Scott Key saw when he got the idea for 'The Star-Spangled Banner.'"

"You mean the bombs bursting in air?" asked Lewis. "Or the rockets' red glare? Because most of the starburst ones were gold, not red."

Rose Rita snorted. "Tell you what," she said. "Let's ask your uncle if he'll conjure up the bombardment of Fort McHenry some time. I think it'd be kind of fun to see Francis Key on board the British ship *Tonnant*, looking to see if the American flag was flying."

Suddenly Lewis had a feeling as if a million ants were running up his spine. Military illusions were one of Uncle Jonathan's magical specialties. He had showed them scenes of Napoleon, Lord Nelson, and General Ulysses S. Grant. Lewis had enjoyed watching the spectacle of the Spanish Armada and others, but now . . . He took a deep, shaky breath. "Maybe. Not right away, though. Somehow I think this summer is a bad time for magic, even if it is only illusions."

Mansion Street was quite dark, with yellow pools of light under the street lamps. Lewis could see Rose Rita only as a silhouette. She turned toward him and said, "You're thinking about that oddball picture."

"Yes, I am," Lewis said. "And the parchment. And that vanishing island. Something bad is getting ready to happen. I can feel it."

They came to Rose Rita's house. "Well, count me in if you need help," she said. "But if I were you, I'd let Mrs.

Zimmermann handle it. She knows all about this stuff, remember. Want to play some flies and grounders tomorrow?"

"I guess," said Lewis. Rose Rita went inside, and Lewis plodded on, sticking his hands into his jeans pockets and walking fast, with his head down. Now that he was alone in the dark, he could imagine danger all around. Lewis felt he should whistle to ward off the danger, like someone whistling past a graveyard. But he was too timid. The sound might attract the attention of something bad. He wanted to be home again, safe in his own house.

At the corner he thought he heard a soft rustling behind him. He turned and looked back, peering into the darkness and hearing the blood pound in his ears. But nothing seemed to be there.

As he climbed the hill, Lewis saw someone standing beneath a streetlight halfway up the slope. It looked like a woman. At first he thought it might be Mrs. Zimmermann. But then he noticed that the figure wore a long black dress and a black veil. Lewis had never seen Mrs. Zimmermann in anything but her favorite color, purple. He slowed down, wondering who this stranger could be.

She must have heard his footsteps, because she looked toward him and took a step back. Lewis breathed a sigh of relief. She looked as timid as he felt. He decided to hurry on past her.

Just as he reached the circle of light beneath the street lamp, the woman spoke to him in a tentative, low voice: "Young man? May I ask you something?"

Lewis edged away. He had always heard you weren't

supposed to talk to strangers, but it seemed impolite just to run past her. Besides, her voice sounded a little worried. Probably she just needed directions. "Y-yes?" he said.

"Do you think I'm pretty?" asked the woman, and reaching up, she tore the veil away.

Lewis felt rooted to the spot. The woman's eyes were burning. But her mouth—her mouth! It was a red gash straight across her face, from ear to ear. It split open, revealing dozens of sharp, curving, yellow teeth. They grinned at Lewis in a horrible leer!

Lewis bolted, running for his life. He heard the woman laugh, and he cast a terrified glance back over his shoulder. She had not moved. She stood beneath the streetlight, her terrible mouth gaping as she laughed and laughed. Then, somehow, she seemed to shimmer, the way the island had just before it vanished. Her figure shrank in on itself until there was nothing there but skin and bone. And the black dress became matted black hair. The creature from the engraving stood there for a second, then leaped forward, becoming part of the night!

Lewis ran with more speed than he thought he had. He banged through the gate at 100 High Street, dashed across the porch, and slammed the front door behind him. He bolted it and leaned back, his chest heaving. "Uncle Jonathan!" he yelled. "Uncle Jonathan, come quick!"

There was no answer. In the darkened foyer Lewis reached for the light switch. His hand hit something that swayed away from him and crashed to the floor with a muffled thud. Lewis found the switch. Weak yellow light flooded the little room. He blinked down at a fallen coat rack.

His uncle didn't have a coat rack. Lewis looked around wildly. The hat stand was gone. The ivory wallpaper with the faint green stripes had vanished. In its place was a deep maroon wallpaper with an intricate pattern of curving vines that wove around white shields. On each shield, in ornate letters, were the initials "II," like the Roman numeral for 2.

Lewis had seen that paper before. It had been on the walls when he first moved to his uncle's house, but Jonathan Barnavelt had long since ripped it all down.

The initials in the shields stood for "Isaac Izard," the evil magician who had once owned the mansion.

Lewis's only thought was to run next door to Mrs. Zimmermann's house. He needed help, and fast. He unbolted the door and threw it open.

Facing him, its twisted body bent so that its wicked face was on a level with his own, was the nightmare from the engraving. It snarled, its yellow eyes blazing. With a wordless shriek, Lewis fled, running up the stairs. He heard a hiss of breath and a shuffle of claws on the wood floor behind him. At the top of the stairs he ran into his own bedroom.

Only it wasn't.

His bed and other furniture were nowhere in sight. Instead there was an ancient mahogany table with legs carved to look like a lion's. Piled all over it were books that were dusty and crumbling. An old-fashioned reading lamp was burning, casting feeble yellow light across the room.

A tarnished brass telescope stood at one window, and an empty chair was in front of that. Lewis realized the thing behind him was probably halfway up the stairs. He would be trapped here!

He dashed out into the darkened hall. The door that should have led to his uncle's room was locked. Lewis thought he heard something behind him. He rushed to the south wing and the second staircase. He ran onto the landing and slammed the door behind him.

This was different too. Halfway down the stairs was an oval window. Lewis knew it as an enchanted one, because his uncle had cast a spell on it to make it show different scenes. Now, though, it was just a clear window through which a little light leaked. Lewis could not find the light switch. He blundered up the stairs in the dark, with some notion of hiding up in the disused rooms.

On the third floor he heard it.

He could not for a moment trust his ears.

The sound was quick and low, and he had heard it years before.

It was the ominous ticking of a clock.

Lewis sobbed. This wasn't fair! He knew that sound. It was the ticking of the Doomsday Clock hidden in the very walls of 100 High Street by the devilish Isaac Izard. But Lewis had smashed the clock. He had thrown it to the floor seconds before the ghost of Selenna Izard could get her hands on it!

Another sound came, the hollow boom of the stairwell door being thrown open below. The monster was on the south stairs! Lewis knew it was hunting for him!

He ran down the hall. Ahead of him, on his right, was a door into a room that Jonathan Barnavelt had locked a long time ago. It was the room beneath the tower of the mansion. Jonathan had said it was Isaac Izard's observatory room. From here the old wizard had studied cloud formations and had plotted the coming of doomsday.

That door burst open!

Lewis stumbled to a stop, one hand on the wall to keep himself from collapsing. A bent old man leered at him. He stood with one hand high on the doorjamb, the other on the doorknob. "You're too late!" cackled the man in a hateful, sneering voice. "I call time! Time's run out! Time and punishment! Time and a grin! Time, time, time, in a sort of runic rhyme! Look at the clock! Where's the big hand, the little hand, and the hand of fate? Too late, too late! Time to strike! Time to kill! The world will know the wrath of the Izards!" His voice rose to a terrible, high-pitched shriek that made water come to Lewis's eyes. He could not understand half of what he heard, but the words seemed to swirl in his mind like a menacing whirlwind.

The stairwell door behind Lewis banged open. Cold air washed over him, smelling horribly of decay and rot. Lewis wanted to run, but he had nowhere to go. He felt something hairy brush the back of his neck—

The world spun around. Lewis screamed and passed out.

CHAPTER SIX

"Lewis? Lewis, can you hear me?" The voice was thin and distant. It sounded as if Lewis were hearing it through cotton. He felt something cool on his forehead—the touch of the terrible hairy creature?

His eyes flew open, and with a yelp of alarm he tried to spring to his feet. Hands on his shoulders held him down. "Easy! Easy!"

Then the room swam into focus. His own room, with its tall mirror, four-poster bed, and familiar rug, black marble fireplace, and bookshelves. And he lay in his bed. Uncle Jonathan was bending over him, his hands on Lewis's shoulders. Beside him stood Mrs. Zimmermann, an anxious look on her face.

"Uncle Jonathan!" cried Lewis, throwing his arms around his uncle's neck. "I thought—"

Jonathan patted his back soothingly. "You're all right, Lewis. But you gave us quite a scare. What happened to you up there?"

Lewis lay back, putting a hand to his forehead. A cool wet washcloth had been placed across it. "Up . . . there?"

Mrs. Zimmermann said, "Jonathan heard you scream from somewhere upstairs. He tore through the whole second floor, but you weren't there. So he went to the third floor, and there you lay, right in front of the parlor that old Isaac Izard used as a cloud observatory."

Lewis gripped his coverlet. Now it came flooding back, the whole horrible evening. He stammered out the story, forgetting that Jonathan knew nothing of the Solomon engraving or of the parchment slip covered in runes.

But Mrs. Zimmermann filled in those details. Jonathan sat at the foot of Lewis's bed and ran a hand through his red hair, making it stand up like a frayed copper brush. "This sounds pretty serious. Something really put a whammy on you, Lewis. When you got home, you saw the house as it was back in, oh, 1940 or so."

"It wasn't real?" asked Lewis with a gulp. "The old man, the monster, none of it?"

Jonathan patted his leg. "Not real in the ordinary sense. The old man you described was Isaac Izard, all right—but you know what he looked like, because you once saw a picture of him. Remember?"

Lewis nodded. "But, gosh, Uncle Jonathan, he seemed real. You don't think h-he—that he—?"

Mrs. Zimmermann seemed to understand. "That he rose from the grave? Not a chance of that! I'm pretty good at sensing the operation of magic, and there hasn't been any in this house lately. Except for your uncle's tomfoolery, of course, but that's got a sort of warm, happy feel to it, not the cold, edgy feel of evil magic at work. Anyway, Lewis, Isaac Izard really wasn't any great shakes as a magician. Oh, he created the Doomsday Clock, I'll grant you, but he just followed an ancient formula for that. His own magic was mainly tied up in trying to prophesy the future from cloud formations. The real wizard in that family was his wife, the late unlamented Selenna."

Uncle Jonathan grimaced. "And both of them are dead and gone, Lewis. Oh, Selenna had enough oomph to have a weird sort of half life for a while, even after she was put in her tomb, but we took the wind out of her sails. No one returns twice from the other side. No, someone just wants us to think that old Isaac is up to his nefarious tricks again. Our problem is to find out who that *someone* is."

Mrs. Zimmermann was looking thoughtful, tapping a finger on her chin. "Hmm. You know, Lewis, that horrible-looking woman you described has a name. She's called *Kuchisake Onna.*"

"Huh?" asked Jonathan. "Hootchy-kootchy Anna?"

"*Kuchisake Onna*, Brush Mush," replied Mrs. Zimmermann tartly. "That's Japanese, as it so happens. It means Big-Mouth Woman. She's not exactly a ghost. More like an evil spirit, something like the Scottish banshee. Except *Kuchisake Onna* doesn't warn people of doom. Instead, she's supposed to bring misfortune when she appears. But I have never heard of her showing up anywhere except in Japan. That seems very curious to me. I wonder if—"

The telephone rang from downstairs. "That might be your overseas call, Florence," said Uncle Jonathan.

"I'll see if it is," said Mrs. Zimmermann.

"Can we go too?" Lewis asked in a small voice. "I'd feel better if all three of us were in the same room."

His uncle raised an eyebrow. "Do you feel up to it?"

"I think so," Lewis told him.

They found Mrs. Zimmermann on the phone downstairs. She was speaking German, which Lewis could not understand. She talked for several minutes, then hung up.

"Well, Frizzy Wig," said Jonathan, "that's going to cost me a fortune! A transatlantic call doesn't go for peanuts, you know."

"It was worth every penny," shot back Mrs. Zimmermann. "That was Professor Athanasius, Professor Emeritus of the Magical Arts from the University of Göttingen in Germany. Though he's retired now, he still has contacts all over the world. I asked him to do some snooping. And he's found out enough to make me think we may be up against one of the Izards, after all."

Jonathan looked troubled. "But Selenna can't rise from the dead a second time, and her husband didn't have the kind of power she commanded."

Mrs. Zimmermann raised a thin finger. "True enough. But they were not the only ones in their wicked family, as it turns out. Years and years ago, back around 1900, they had a son."

"I knew that," said Jonathan. "But I thought he died when he was still an infant."

Mrs. Zimmermann sighed. "So did we all. But Professor Athanasius says that in 1922—the same year I got my doctorate in magic—a certain Ishmael Izard arrived in Austria from England. He was just a young fellow, between twenty and twenty-five years old. He had been studying magic in Cornwall with a minor wizard named Karswell or something like that. In Austria he became an apprentice to Hans Horbiger."

Jonathan let out a low, surprised whistle. "Could that young man have been Isaac's son?"

Mrs. Zimmermann shrugged. "Isaac and Selenna's bouncing baby boy was christened Ishmael, and the one who turned up in Austria in 1922 was an American and exactly the right age. And you know what Hans Horbiger was like."

"What was he like?" asked Lewis, not sure he even wanted to know.

Mrs. Zimmermann gave him a reassuring smile. "Horbiger was an astrologer who dabbled in magic and who had tons of nutty theories, including one that the whole universe was made of ice. But he had lots of connections among European sorcerers, and Ishmael Izard learned from many of them. Izard left Austria in 1930, and—get this, Jonathan—traveled to Japan, where he studied Asian magic under an Ainu tutor for ten years."

"That would explain the *Kuchisake Onna* Lewis saw," Jonathan said. "I'll bet you dollars to doughnuts, French fries to francs, and marshmallows to marks that she was an illusion whomped up just to terrify Lewis."

"I wouldn't take that bet," replied Mrs. Zimmermann, "because I'm about ninety-nine and forty-four-one-hundredths percent convinced that you're right. Well, just before World War Two our fine-feathered fiend Ishmael disappeared from view. But Professor Athanasius thinks he's been globe-trotting ever since. You see, all over the world little oddball communities of sorcerers have sprung up in the last twelve or thirteen years. Nobody knows much about them, but a lot of good magicians are concerned. There may be twenty-five or thirty of these communities, each one with forty or fifty members."

"Evil magicians, eh?" said Jonathan with a scowl. "And what are they up to?"

"Absolutely nothing," said Mrs. Zimmermann. "At least, nothing that anyone can pin down. They seem to be practicing magic, but not using it for anything in particular. Unless, of course, they're channeling it to you-know-who."

"What do you mean?" asked Lewis, feeling helpless and confused.

Jonathan shook his head. "Frizzy Wig means, Lewis, that little bunches of these rotten apples may be brewing up some bad magic. But instead of using it themselves, they're sending it to Ishmael Izard. He's like, oh, like a toaster or an electric fan. He plugs into that flow of magic, and suddenly he's the top dog. He's got more power than any one magician ordinarily could control or handle. But I don't understand—what do the bad guys get out of this? I've never known an evil magician yet that didn't have some selfish reason for doing his misdeeds!"

"Now, that I can't tell you," admitted Mrs. Zimmermann. "Lord knows what mischief they're planning. But I have a sneaky suspicion that we've stepped into the middle of something extremely nasty. I'm beginning to be able to guess about some things. Jonathan, I don't think you tripped and fell into your cellar. I think someone was poking around down there, searching for a trace of the Doomsday Clock that Selenna Izard tried to wind up. Maybe he didn't know that Lewis had smashed it to bits."

"That would explain a lot," reflected Jonathan grimly. "If Ishmael thought he could pick up that terrifying timepiece and start it tick-tocking again, he just might have been looking for it in the cellar. And a magician who can conjure up hallucinations and apparitions wouldn't have had much trouble making me think I heard Lewis."

"So it's possible he was here and after the clock," mused Mrs. Zimmermann. "Fortunately for us and for the world, the clock is gone beyond repair."

"But what if he's making a new one?" asked Lewis.

Jonathan and Mrs. Zimmermann exchanged a long look. Mrs. Zimmermann said, "Lewis, that's what we're worried about. I can think of three reasons why Ishmael Izard might have wanted to get his hands on the Doomsday Clock. One, he wanted to wind it up fully and bring on the end of the world himself, as his twisted father tried to do. Two, he knew what the blasted thing could do and wanted to destroy it to protect the world. Or three, he wanted to stop it from running because he was creating a similar spell himself, and he knew that two spells based on the same kind of magic can cancel each other out."

Lewis swallowed hard. "M-maybe he was sorry for

what his father tried to do. Maybe he just wanted to make sure the clock was destroyed."

Jonathan shook his head. "We can't assume that, I'm afraid. I don't think an innocent person would sneak around like that. And I'm certain that anyone who meant no harm wouldn't scare you out of your skin the way someone did tonight, Lewis. Hmm. These things have a strange way of looking like coincidences. Florence, do you think our odd experience up on Lake Superior might tie in to all this?"

"It's possible," agreed Mrs. Zimmermann. "After all, someone knew that Lewis was up on Ivarhaven Island. They had to, to send him the picture and the slip of parchment."

"Right," said Jonathan. "By the way, Lewis, have you hung on to that little love letter?"

"It's in my wallet," Lewis said. He pulled it from his jeans pocket, opened it, and took out the yellowish-white slip of parchment. He started to unfold it.

Suddenly the material seemed to come to life. It wriggled disgustingly in Lewis's hand. With a cry of alarm, Lewis flung it away. The parchment streaked for an open window, hit the screen, and fluttered wildly, like a moth beating its wings frantically, trying to escape. Mrs. Zimmermann sprang up at once. "Don't let it get away!" she yelled.

Jonathan lunged to the window. The parchment had found the edge of the screen and was trying to worm its way through the tiny gap between the screen and the windowsill. With a loud slap, Jonathan clapped his hands over it. He pulled it away from the window. For a moment it writhed visibly in his grip. Lewis had the strange impression that it was furious, that it was filled with hatred for them all.

The moment passed. The parchment hung limply from Jonathan's fingers. He unfolded it, looked carefully at the markings on it, and then returned it to Lewis. "Be very careful with this," he warned. "I agree with Florence: Your safety may depend on your treating this very protectively. Keep it in your wallet, and don't take it out unless Florence or I ask you to. Understood?"

Lewis crammed the parchment back into his wallet and hastily thrust the wallet into his jeans pocket. "Understood," he said in a voice that squeaked with dread.

Jonathan put his big hand on Lewis's shoulder. "Don't worry," he declared. "No matter what Ishmael Izard, or Dirty Dan, or Seven-Toed Pete, or whatever he calls himself is up to, we'll see it through together. The three of us will fix his wagon, all right."

"The four of us," said a voice from the front door.

Jonathan started, and they all spun around. Rose Rita stood in the doorway, her face very pale. "Something came scratching at my window as I was getting ready for bed," she said. "I turned a flashlight on it, but all I could see were two glowing yellow eyes. Then it ran away from the window."

"You saw it?" gasped Lewis. "Why didn't you call me?"

"I couldn't," confessed Rose Rita, sounding miserable. "My mom and dad were still up watching TV, and the phone's in the living room. But I got dressed, and as soon as I could, I slipped outside. I wanted to make sure you were okay, so I ran over."

Lewis gave her a shaky smile. He knew that he would never have had the courage to go chasing off into the night like that. Not after having seen the dark shape with the glowing eyes! "Thanks," he said.

Rose Rita nodded and then tilted her head as she looked at Mrs. Zimmermann and Uncle Jonathan. "I heard some of what you were saying. It's that picture someone sent Lewis, isn't it?"

"Yes," said Mrs. Zimmermann. "Along with other things. But it may be dangerous, dear."

"I don't care!" returned Rose Rita fiercely. "Nobody is going to push us around like this!"

Jonathan threw back his head and gave his great, booming laugh. "I'd hate to have Rose Rita mad at me!" he announced. "All right, then. One for all, and all for one! We'll be the Four Musketeers of magic, and we'll soon find out what's what. Now there's one important thing left to do."

"What's that?" asked Mrs. Zimmermann. "Say the word!"

Jonathan grinned. "Why, Pruny Face! You have to go bring over the chocolate cake I happen to know you baked today. We all need a midnight snack to get our energy up!"

Lewis didn't think he could eat a bite. Somehow, though, once Mrs. Zimmermann did in fact bring over her delicious chocolate cake, he managed to pack away two big pieces.

CHAPTER SEVEN

Weeks passed. Jonathan and Mrs. Zimmermann spent a lot of time making sure that no evil lurked in the Barnavelt house. Rose Rita volunteered to help, and she and Lewis pitched in. The effort was monumental. The four began in the basement. They had to make sure that the passage where the Doomsday Clock had been hidden contained no secrets.

After several hours of probing and searching, Mrs. Zimmermann announced that it was clear. "No booby traps, tiger pits, or ticking time bombs," she stated with weary cheerfulness. "Heaven knows why this thing was built originally. It certainly is just as old as the house, which means that it wasn't put here by Isaac Izard. My hunch is that the original builder started to create a storm cellar here but never got around to finishing it. Or maybe it was supposed to be a wine cellar. Anyway, there's nothing sinister lurking here."

But that was only the beginning of the search. At Uncle Jonathan's insistence, they went through the house from attic to cellar, hauling tons of useless old junk out. "What will the neighbors think?" fretted Mrs. Zimmermann as the pile of discarded old bureaus, broken chairs, moth-eaten curtains, and threadbare sofas mounted at the curb.

"They'll think crazy old Barnavelt finally got around to spring-cleaning," chuckled Jonathan. "Even if it is July!"

For Lewis the worst part of the whole week came when Jonathan unlocked the door on the third floor. It led into the old parlor where Isaac Izard had once sat for days on end, studying cloud formations through the big front window. Izard, a bitter and angry man, had decided that the whole world was against him. In revenge he planned to end the world. Of course, that would mean that he ended himself too, but as Mrs. Zimmermann observed, "Old Droopy Drawers hated this world so much that he was willing to swap for the next one."

"He must have had a screw loose," Rose Rita added, puffing under the weight of a rolled-up carpet.

"Of course he did," returned Jonathan. "He was loony, nutty, and touched in the head. But that made him more dangerous, if anything. Luckily, he was also indecisive." He went on to explain that Izard knew a spell to end the world. It would not even require a Doomsday Clock. But he had to say it at just the right moment, and he could know the right moment only when he saw certain cloud formations.

"That happened twice," continued Jonathan as they lugged the carpet out to the curb. "Twice over a forty-two year period of watching and waiting. But clouds change fast, you know. By the time Isaac was sure he had seen the right cloud formations, they had broken up. That's what convinced him to set the Doomsday Clock a-ticking. But as luck would have it, his magic wasn't the right kind to wind it up fully. Only his wife, Selenna, could have done that, and she died before the clock was finished."

They heaved the carpet onto the mountain of junk. It landed with a *flump!* and a choking cloud of dust. Lewis coughed and backed away from it. "Could we not talk about it?" he asked. "When I think about the Izards, I get so that every time I go inside, I think I hear that clock ticking."

"Okay," agreed his uncle cheerfully. "No more Izard talk. Now, I think with maybe two more trips, we'll have cleared out the third floor. . . ."

Of course they didn't clear the third floor out completely. Jonathan was a pack rat, and he kept all the really interesting stuff. They turned up thousands of stereopticon photos—pictures taken in the 1800's. When you put them into a special viewer and peered through it, you saw a brown, three-dimensional world. There were circus scenes and pictures of Cape Cod, jungle scenes and the New York harbor before the Statue of Liberty was there, the Himalayan mountains and kittens chasing a ball of twine. They stored all these photos in huge cardboard boxes and took only a little time to look at some of them. Jonathan kept the parlor organs too, and any furniture that looked more like an antique than like junk.

Mrs. Zimmermann helped, and she used a crystal ball to make sure they turned up no magical items, no evil influences. Twice during the week Jute Feasel, who worked for the Capharnaum County Public Works Department, drove up with a big dump truck to take away all the stuff they were discarding. Jute looked at the mountain of trash, cursed colorfully, and then hauled it all off, leaving behind a cloud of King Edward cigar smoke.

Finally, on a rainy afternoon toward the middle of July, Jonathan, Mrs. Zimmermann, Rose Rita, and Lewis all sat around the kitchen table. They were exhausted and grimy. Mrs. Zimmermann had smudges of dust on her nose and cheek. Uncle Jonathan was sweaty, with his red hair plastered to his forehead and even his red beard limp. "Well," he rumbled, "mission accomplished. Whatever the source of this nasty spell is, it doesn't begin here."

"But at least we've finally given this mossy old manse the cleaning it's needed for years," said Mrs. Zimmermann. Distant thunder growled outside. She looked upward. "I hope all the windows are closed."

Jonathan nodded. "They are. All right, we've just about busted a gut—"

Mrs. Zimmermann, who was once a schoolteacher, winced. "Jonathan, please!"

Rose Rita laughed, and Jonathan winked at her. "Very well, Florence. We have very nearly perforated our internal integuments, with no luck. I suggest that the next step is to go back to Ivarhaven Island and check out the strange things that happened there."

Mrs. Zimmermann drummed her fingers on the table. "I'm not convinced it would do much good. Albert reports—"

"You've been in touch with Grampa Galway?" asked Rose Rita, sounding surprised.

"I certainly have," Mrs. Zimmermann said. "Albert doesn't know that I'm a witch, to be sure, and he doesn't know about Jonathan's sorcery. But he does know that the weird island we landed on somehow isn't right. And he's on the spot and in the best place to keep an eye on things."

"What about the island?" asked Lewis, whose nightmares were beginning to feature the sinister dark tower looming above the trees.

With a shake of her head, Mrs. Zimmermann said, "Nothing, really, Lewis. Albert reports no more materializations of the place, and he hasn't found anyone else in the area who wants to talk about it. He has double-checked the charts and maps, and an island that size doesn't show up on any of them. In fact, as far as he can tell, the place where the island is should be marked by one rather big, unlovely rock sticking up above the waves. He can't even find that."

Rose Rita pushed her glasses up and rubbed her eyes. "Maybe just anyone can't see the island," she suggested. "Maybe we could see it because we had two magicians on the boat."

Jonathan and Mrs. Zimmermann gave each other an astonished look. "Of course!" bellowed Jonathan, pounding his right fist into his left palm. "Rose Rita, you're a genius! What do you think, Florence?"

"It could be!" said Mrs. Zimmermann, her voice excited. "It could very well be! If the island is protected by a magical field—or if it doesn't even belong to our world—"

Lewis didn't like the sound of all this. "How could it not belong to the world? We walked on it! It wasn't something we imagined!"

Mrs. Zimmermann smiled reassuringly. "Oh, it was real enough, Lewis. But it's like—well, this is very hard to explain. You know how two soap bubbles will touch and suddenly stick together? Well, imagine for a moment that the universe we know isn't the only universe. Maybe there are lots of them. And at times, two of them might touch and for a moment stick together at the point where they meet, like two soap bubbles. At such places, something that is not really part of our world might appear in our world."

Rose Rita said slowly, "It's really part of the other universe, but it's right at the point where they stick together."

"Correct," said Uncle Jonathan. "Now, I'm no scientist, but I know that people like Professor Albert Einstein think such things are possible. But because their business is science, not magic, they don't know that a powerful magician might be able to call the two soap bubbles together and hold them there. Maybe a scientist would say that the island we saw is part of another dimension.

Maybe it's a part of our world, but it's in the wrong time. It could have existed before the last Ice Age, or maybe it's from five thousand years in the future. When we went through that shimmery barrier, we might have gone backward in time, or forward."

"Or sideways, or inside out and upside down," put in Mrs. Zimmermann. "The truth is, we don't know. We have a strong suspicion, though, that the island doesn't belong to our world. It's here through some kind of magic, and that's what we have to check out."

Lewis's heart was beating a little too fast. "But if it takes a magician to even see the island, that means—"

"We'll have to go back," said Jonathan gently. "Or at least one of us will."

"No!" yelled Lewis. "My gosh, Uncle Jonathan, Mrs. Zimmermann says that practically every bad wizard in the world is shooting power to Ishmael Izard! You could get killed!"

Mrs. Zimmermann sighed. "That is not what I meant, Lewis. Ishmael Izard—if indeed it is he—has some followers scattered across the world. Perhaps he has hundreds of them. Still, that is far from 'every bad wizard in the world.' And believe me, Jonathan and I know all about the dangers involved. We plan to be very, very careful indeed."

"Both of you?" wailed Lewis. "And you're gonna ditch me here?"

"No one's going to 'ditch' you, Lewis," his uncle told him patiently. He thought for a minute. "Actually, Lewis has a good point, Florence. There's no reason for both of us to go tearing up to Ivarhaven Island. We could be wrong. Maybe the Final Hour isn't what this is all about. Someone should stay here and keep a finger on the pulse of things. And since you have people all over the globe reporting to you, it makes sense that I should go."

Lewis felt like bursting into tears. Wouldn't anyone listen to him? Mrs. Zimmermann made a tutting sound with her tongue. "You wouldn't be equipped to handle anything really bad, you know," she reminded Jonathan. "As you yourself say, you're really more of a parlor magician. Whereas I can call on some pretty powerful enchantment if push comes to shove."

"Before anyone starts pushing or shoving," said Jonathan, "we have to find the island first. And I think my magic is at least strong enough to let me detect any ordinary spell of concealment."

Lewis couldn't stand it. He slipped off his chair and went into the front parlor. Rose Rita followed him. "They're going to leave us out," she said grimly. "I know they are."

Lewis rested his chin on his hand. "They think they're protecting us."

Rose Rita sat on the sofa and crossed her arms. "Well, I don't know about you, but I'm not going to put up with it. I'm going to tell my mom and dad that Grampa wants me to come up to the island and help him out around the house. Mom worries about him a lot. I think she'd let me go on the bus, especially if Grampa was expecting me."

Lewis stared at her in disbelief. Was Rose Rita planning to abandon him too? "But Ishmael Izard and his magic—I mean, what if something happens?"

Rose Rita shrugged. "My folks don't know anything about old Whosis and his magical whammy," she pointed out. "So they won't worry. And I plan to be very extra-special careful. I won't let anything happen to me!"

None of that helped Lewis's feelings. "I'll be left here by myself," he said unhappily.

Shaking her head, Rose Rita said, "No, you won't. Either your uncle will stay, or Mrs. Zimmermann will. Now I've got to call Grampa and persuade him to ask my folks to let me come up for the rest of the summer. That shouldn't be hard. He always says I'm his favorite relative!" Suddenly Rose Rita gave Lewis a stern look. "Hey, you've got to keep this quiet, understand? If your uncle or Mrs. Zimmermann found out what I'm planning, they'd be sure to heave a monkey wrench into the works."

"I don't know," began Lewis. "It seems wrong—"

"Look, Lewis," Rose Rita pointed out, "we've got to keep an eye on whoever goes up there. I know you wouldn't want your uncle to be snooping around that mysterious island when nobody knew where he was going or what he was trying to do. And I certainly want Mrs. Zimmermann to be safe. I know it's kind of lousy of me to run off and leave you here, but somebody's got to go. And because my grampa is already there, I'm the logical choice. Promise me you won't say anything?"

Unwillingly, Lewis muttered, "Okay. I promise."

Before many days had passed, everything fell into

place. Uncle Jonathan would go to the Upper Peninsula and see what he could discover about the vanishing island. Lewis would stay in Mrs. Zimmermann's guest room and help her research the spells and magic that might provide protection.

And, though neither of the adults knew it, Rose Rita would leave for Porcupine Bay on a Greyhound bus a whole day before Uncle Jonathan got started. When he arrived, she would already be on hand. She promised Lewis that she would stay in touch and let him know of any developments.

That left Lewis worried and far from satisfied. Still, it was the best they could do, and he had to settle for it. On Saturday morning, he stood on the curb in front of his house and waved as his uncle drove away in his boxy old Muggins Simoon. As he watched the car chug down the hill, Lewis couldn't help wondering if he would ever see his uncle—or Rose Rita—alive again.

CHAPTER EIGHT

That same night, much to Lewis's surprise, Jonathan telephoned from Porcupine Bay to say he had arrived. It was about half past nine when Mrs. Zimmermann answered the phone. She handed the receiver to Lewis, who heard his uncle's voice.

"That was sure a fast trip," Lewis said.

His uncle chortled. "Let's say I made a beeline for the Upper Peninsula. Don't worry. I was careful and didn't break any speed limits. Not badly, anyway. Despite what Florence says, there's plenty of life in the old Simoon, and I am a pretty good driver. And since I didn't stop to eat, I made very good time, thank you. Speaking of Florence, I need to talk to her again."

Lewis handed the phone back to Mrs. Zimmermann.

After a short, soft conversation, she hung up and smiled at Lewis. His expression must have showed how anxious he was, because in a reassuring voice, Mrs. Zimmermann said, "Lewis, please don't worry. Your uncle can take care of himself, and he's fine. Jonathan says he's found a little fishing cabin to rent up there in Porcupine Bay—"

"He's not staying with Mr. Galway?" asked Lewis, blinking in surprise. He had just assumed that Jonathan would go back to the mansion on Ivarhaven Island.

Mrs. Zimmermann shook her head. "No. He doesn't want to impose on Albert, and anyway, Jonathan thinks he can snoop around more if he's on the mainland." She yawned. "I beg your pardon! I haven't been getting enough sleep lately, what with Izards and wizards and Final Hours and mysterious towers spinning around in my head! I promised Jonathan I'd see you got to Mass tomorrow morning, but after that, we can collect Rose Rita and run down to my cottage on Lyon Lake. I want to make sure that the carpenters I hired did a good job of taking down that wobbly old pier next to my property. It'll be fun to combine a picnic with my tour of inspection."

Lewis felt uncomfortable. "Okay. Only I don't think Rose Rita can go. She said something about going out of town." After a pause, Lewis added, "With her family." It was true, in a way, he thought. Grampa Galway *was* part of her family. But Lewis was all too aware of how weak his excuse sounded, and of how his uncertain voice made it all the worse. He was no good at this kind of secrecy. Rose

Rita was the one with the vivid imagination and the quick wit. Lewis had a hard time telling a simple fib or even keeping a secret.

To his relief, Mrs. Zimmermann didn't seem to notice. "Very well," she said. "Then you and I will make the trip. I'll bake us a cake and we'll have a regular picnic and laze away the afternoon." She fought back another yawn, and then smiled in a sleepy way. "But right now I'm going to bundle myself off to bed. Don't stay up too late reading."

"I won't," promised Lewis. In fact, he had already finished the book he had been reading, a rousing sea adventure by C. S. Forester. He thought briefly of going next door and getting another book from his room, but then he stared at the dark windows. The night was black. Lewis couldn't help shivering. He knew he lacked the courage even to cross the yard when the hairy *thing* might be lurking out there.

Maybe he could find something to read in Mrs. Zimmermann's house. Lewis went to a plain walnut bookshelf that stood against one wall of the front parlor. Its shelves were crammed with dozens of volumes. Most of the books were about magic, but some of the newer ones on the top shelf were about travel to exotic places. One was partly pulled out from its place. Lewis tilted his head to read the title on the book's spine: *Celtic Lands and Peoples*. Curious, he pulled it out.

The pages fell open at a bookmark. Only, Lewis saw, it wasn't really a bookmark at all, but a smudgy typewritten letter on the very thin kind of paper called onionskin.

The paper was so flimsy that it was almost transparent. Even with the letter folded, Lewis could make out part of one line: ". . . your young friend Lewis Barnavelt."

Overcome with curiosity, Lewis unfolded the paper and read what it said:

14 July
Goldschmitt Str. 412-B
Göttingen

My dear Dr. Zimmermann:

What a pleasure it was to speak to you again. I have been investigating the runes you have described to me as having been given to your young friend Lewis Barnavelt. Here is a translation, so far as my regrettably faulty knowledge of Celtic runes is capable of making:

> *To Lewis Barnavelt: Azrael is summoned, and his servant of the night is loosed to follow your steps and to number the minutes of life remaining unto you. You are granted forty-eight days.*

As you say, my dear Dr. Zimmermann, this is puzzling in the extreme. However, in an article by Karswell (1890) I have found a reference to a form of sending practised by rogue members of the Temple of Thalestris, and this I fear is an example of such. This is a method of casting the runes, of calling disaster upon the unfortunate who receives it. The mention of Azrael and the servant of the night is particularly troubling. The danger comes, if your statement of the dates is accurate, on 15 August.

I know of no counterspell, but if your young friend can pass the parchment back to the giver, that may keep him from harm. In the meanwhile, impress upon him the utter necessity of keeping the parchment safe. It will struggle to destroy itself, and if it succeeds, he is lost. By the way, in English you will find a fiction about such a spell in the writings of the great ghost-story author M. R. James. It might be worth reading.

If I may for a moment call you Florence and add a personal note, then I must say that I will ask as many of our colleagues as I can find to assist you. Good luck, and if you are ever in Germany, look in on your old friend.

Hermann Athanasius, D.Mag.A.
(Professor Emeritus, Universität Göttingen)

Lewis folded the letter with trembling fingers, and he slid the book back onto the shelf. After a moment of doubtful hesitation, he pulled out another volume from a lower shelf. This was a fat *Encyclopedia of Supernatural and Occult Knowledge*. Its pebbly maroon leather cover felt slippery in his grip. Lewis was breathing so shallowly that he was dizzy. He closed his eyes and tried to force himself to calm down. Then he sat in an armchair with a reading lamp beside it. After gathering his courage once more,

Lewis felt ready. He opened the book to the A's, almost hoping he would not find the entry. But there it was in black and white:

Azrael, Azri'al: In Jewish tradition, the name of one of the fourteen Angels of Death. In Islamic teachings . . .

From the corner of his eye Lewis saw something on the arm of his chair. It was dark, and it was right beside his wrist. The hairs on his arms and the back of his neck prickled. For a terrible second he thought the dark gray splotch was a spider. An enormous spider, like one of the South American tarantulas that preyed on birds.

One of the spider legs moved. And then Lewis realized that the shape might be a hand—a bony, hairy hand—

With a stifled screech, Lewis leaped out of the chair and spun around. The dark shape was nothing more than the shadow of the reading lamp's chain, which ended in a tassel.

But then, the shape in the King Solomon engraving had looked just like a shadow too.

Lewis fumbled the encyclopedia back into its place on the shelf. His teeth chattered as if he were freezing. He ran to the guest bedroom, locked himself in, and drew the curtains over the windows. Jumping into bed fully clothed, he lay there cowering. He tugged the covers over his face and in a hushed voice, he recited a Latin prayer over and over:

"*Nam et si ambulavero in medio umbrae mortis non timebo mala* . . ." It was from the book of Psalms in the Bible, and the words meant "Though I walk in the midst of the shadow of death, I will fear no evil." But Lewis *did* fear. He feared what would happen on August 15. Did he have less than three weeks to live? He was so afraid that he could not go to sleep until very late. So late, in fact, that through the closed curtains he could see the first faint light of dawn.

Then, at last, he fell into a disturbed sleep, his dreams troubled by visions of a sneaking, hairy creature. He could feel its terrible yellow eyes staring at him. Made of shadows and hatred, it hovered at the edge of his vision, and whenever he turned his head, it had vanished. But Lewis knew it was there, just waiting.

The clock was ticking.

He had only until the middle of August before something dreadful happened.

"Rose Rita," said Albert Galway, "I appreciate your wanting to help your old granddad, but you don't seem to be having a good time so far."

They were sitting at the breakfast table early on Sunday morning. Rose Rita sipped her cup of hot chocolate and gave her grandfather a weary smile. "I'm just tired out from that long bus trip. How's everything going?"

"Fine, fine," Mr. Galway said. He took a long drink of coffee. "Heard from Jim Marvin the other day. His yacht has performed well in the trials, so he's going to be in the big race the middle of next month." He shook his bald head. "You know, down in Australia it's winter right now. I wouldn't want to be out on those wild waters in a sailboat, even if it's one of the best. No, I sailed around the Horn and around the Cape of Good Hope, and I know those harsh gales of the roaring forties. Lake Superior is more my speed!"

Rose Rita pushed her fried egg around on her plate. "Did you ever find out anything about that strange island?"

Grampa Galway set his cup down. "Found out the name of it. Maybe. Jake Brannigan—he's the owner of the store over in Porcupine Bay, as well as the postmaster, justice of the peace, and chief cook and bottle-washer—what was I saying? Oh, yes, Jake says that he thinks it might be a place called Gnomon Island. Funny name for an island, if you ask me. There's a fella named Clusko that comes in and picks up mail two, three times a week. Somebody once asked him where he was camping, and he laughed and said Gnomon Island. Nobody in Porcupine Bay's ever heard of it, so Jake figures it might be the one we saw."

"I wonder who built that tower," said Rose Rita, trying to sound casual.

Her grandfather shrugged. "You got me. Might be an old abandoned lighthouse put up by the Coast Guard. Might have been built in ancient days by the Chippewa, for all I know." He frowned. "One thing I do know is that the place felt bad to me. Whoever lives in that cottage doesn't like visitors. I'm not planning on going back, anyway."

Rose Rita didn't think she should push the subject any farther. She got up and said, "I'll do the dishes."

Her grandfather laughed. "Much obliged, matey, but this place has all the modern conveniences." He got up and helped her load the dishwasher. It was the first one that Rose Rita had ever seen, and she immediately decided that one day she would own one. She hated washing dishes.

After cleaning up, the two of them played a couple of games of Hearts. Then Grampa Galway had some chores to do. He left Rose Rita alone in the study, and she sat wondering why Jonathan had not shown up. She knew that he had planned to drive up sometime that weekend. And she wasn't particularly looking forward to seeing him, because she knew very well that he wouldn't approve of her snooping around.

But she also felt that she owed it to Lewis to find out everything she could. Mrs. Zimmermann and Uncle Jonathan would try to protect him, but they would do it the way grown-ups always did. For his own good they would keep things secret from him.

And Rose Rita hated not knowing secrets even worse than she hated washing dishes. She checked her watch. It was only 10:12. She picked up the phone, hesitated, and then dialed zero. When the operator came on, Rose Rita told her she wanted to place a person-to-person long-distance call and gave Mrs. Zimmermann's number, but Lewis's name.

The phone rang only once before Lewis answered: "Hello, Zimmermann residence."

The operator asked if he were Lewis Barnavelt, and when he said yes, she told Rose Rita, "Go ahead, please."

"You alone?" Rose Rita asked in a low voice.

"No," said Lewis.

"Oh. Mrs. Zimmermann's there nearby, huh?"

"That's right."

Rose Rita thought for a moment. It was probably better not to let Mrs. Zimmermann know where she was. "Listen," she told Lewis, "remember what I'm going to tell you, and when you get a chance, write it down so you won't forget. Okay?"

"That'll be fine," said Lewis.

"Okay," replied Rose Rita. "First, the name of the island we saw might be Gnomon Island. I think that's spelled g-n-o-m-o-n, but I could be wrong. Got that?"

"Uh-huh."

"Next, somebody named Clusko might—"

"Wh-what?" demanded Lewis, his voice suddenly tight and high.

"Clusko," repeated Rose Rita. "Have you heard of someone by that name?"

"Uh, right," said Lewis. "In the store."

Rose Rita frowned. "The store in Porcupine Bay, you mean?"

"That first day," added Lewis.

Nearly bouncing out of her chair, Rose Rita said, "You *saw* him?"

She heard Lewis say something too soft to make out, and after a pause, he added quickly, "I told Mrs. Zimmermann I thought I smelled something burning. She's baking a cake. Listen, there was a short little guy in the store when we first drove up there. He had wiry black hair, and he looked kind of creepy. They said his name was Clusko."

"Okay," said Rose Rita. "I'll talk Grampa into going over to the store, and I'll go along and ask some questions. When's your uncle coming up?"

"Already there," Lewis told her. "He's renting a cabin. She's coming back. I'd better go."

"I'll call back tomorrow," promised Rose Rita. She hung up the phone. Despite Lewis's fear and despite her own worries, she smiled. She loved detective shows on radio and on TV, and this was just like a deep, dark mystery. She decided that her next step would be to question the suspects at the general store in Porcupine Bay.

Maybe, she thought, she could even find out about this Clusko and about the mysterious Gnomon Island. It would be great if she could crack the case and tell Jonathan and Mrs. Zimmermann exactly what they had to deal with.

First, though, she'd have to persuade her grandfather that it would be worth a boat trip to run over to Porcupine Bay on a Sunday afternoon. And what if the store wasn't even open?

"I'll cross that bridge when I come to it," Rose Rita told herself. And she set off to do some detecting.

CHAPTER NINE

Late that same afternoon a splintered old red motorboat chugged up to the wooden pier on Gnomon Island. Only one person was in it: a very short man with bushy black hair. He moved in strange jerks. As he tied the boat and climbed out, he darted his head this way and that, as if expecting some enemy would leap at him. He gathered to gether two brown paper bags and hurried up the winding path, running awkwardly on his bandy legs.

He spoke a word at the door of a little cottage, and the door unlocked itself, swinging open on silent hinges. The short man hurried inside. The room he entered was very plain. Two beds stood against the left and right walls. Each was covered by a green Army blanket, and each was made up neatly, with hospital corners. Against the front wall to the man's left, near the door, was a table. On the other side of the door stood a bookcase jammed with ancient-looking tomes. At the back of the room was a wood-burning stove. Pots, pans, and plates were stored on shelves above it. A squat, old-fashioned icebox was against the opposite wall. The only other room was the bathroom.

He stored some bacon and eggs in the icebox and put a loaf of bread and several cans of food on one of the shelves. Then he carefully folded the paper bags and put them in a wooden crate near the stove. He gave the room a last look around and hurried out, pausing outside the door to speak a word that made the door close and lock itself.

For a few minutes he stood in front of the cottage, rubbing his hands together as if he were washing them. He shook his head several times in a dissatisfied, apprehensive way. "I don't like them snooping and spying, I don't," he grumbled to himself. Then he hurried up the hillside, through the trees, following the pathway to the tower.

He stood up there, of course. He stood on the far eastern shoulder of the hill. It was afternoon, and shadows were long. The shadow of the dark tower fell almost at the tall man's feet. But he wasn't looking at his feet. His face was turned toward the east, where piles of clouds reached high into the sky.

"Yes, Mr. Clusko?" the tall man said without even looking at him.

The short man followed one of the curving gravel paths. He wore heavy black brogans, and with each step the gravel crunched under their soles. He stopped a few feet away from the other man. "Sir, the Barnavelt man is back."

The tall man nodded. His hair was iron-gray and he wore it unusually long. It hung down his neck, gleaming in the late sun. "Barnavelt is back. Of course he is. Of course he is."

Clusko licked his lips. "He's asking questions, snooping and spying. You—you're not worried?"

The tall man did not bother to reply. A light breeze ruffled his long hair. His face was craggy in the afternoon light, like a mask roughly chiseled from sandstone. "There," he said, lifting an arm to point upward. "There. You see?"

Clusko looked to the east. The towering clouds had assumed the shape of a monstrous human face. Deep shadows marked the eye sockets. The nose was long and curving, like the beak of a hawk. The mouth was a frowning grimace. Clusko could not help trembling. "It is very like him. Like the pictures I have seen of him, I mean."

"My late lamented father," said the other man. "Isaac Izard. It's fading already."

The clouds were always in movement. The left half of the face crumpled. The right eye socket folded itself outward, like a flower blooming. In five minutes no face could be seen.

Ishmael Izard sighed. "He dreamed of so much power, and yet he ended with nothing. Do you know where he failed?"

Clusko bowed his head. No matter what he answered, it would be wrong. "No," he murmured.

"Of course not," said Izard in a voice of scorn. "How could you? You are nothing but a failed wizard yourself, after all. If you understood the reasons for failure, you would not have lost so badly. To think such a thing as you challenged me to a duel of magic! You are lucky I even allowed you to live, much less accepted you as my servant so you might witness my greatest work."

"Yes, sir," whispered Clusko through clenched teeth.

Izard sniffed. "My father thought to end the world because he was dissatisfied with his share in it. Foolish, foolish! The world holds many pleasant things in it. Unfortunately, it holds many possessive people as well. But that will change. The signs are in the sky even now. When the time is right, when the Clock brings a day of darkness, then how all things will alter! What will you be in the new world? Still nothing more than my servant, of course. But your master will then be the emperor of all. This crowded globe will be swept clear of all inferior beings. Only my followers will survive. And I, I will be their master."

"But Barnavelt has come—"

"Barnavelt is nothing!" The words came like the lash of a whip. "A parlor magician! He is weak in power, weaker in knowledge and understanding. He shall suffer when the time comes. No quick death for him! What you do not understand, my poor Clusko, is that I want him here. Yes, and the more powerful witch Zimmermann as well, and that cursed boy who thwarted my mother's plan—"

"But if he had not, the world would have ended," whined Clusko. "Ended before your own scheme had come to anything."

"Oh, so you believe I should thank this Lewis Barnavelt?" snarled Izard. "Be grateful to the little devil who called my mother back from the tomb, then banished her forever? No, no, he must suffer too. And he will suffer most horribly. The runes will take care of that."

For some time the two said nothing. The swollen red sun sank in the west, touched the horizon, and then slowly vanished. When only a broad crimson glow was left, Izard scanned the sky once more. "No more clouds. No more signs." But then he chuckled. "One more day gone. Soon, Clusko, soon. My trap is baited. The clock is running. And this time the fools cannot even see it!"

In the gathering darkness the failed wizard Clusko shivered again.

After a week of rainy weather, the sky finally cleared over Ivarhaven Island. On a hot Monday afternoon near the end of July Rose Rita finally found someone she could really talk to. Her name was Marta Krebsmeyer, and she was twelve and a half years old. Marta's dad was a fishing guide in Porcupine Bay, and her mom was a teacher. Marta herself was bored. "Sure, there's lots for *tourists* to do here," she told Rose Rita scornfully as they tossed a baseball back and forth on the playground of Porcupine Bay Combined School. Marta was a chunky girl with short dark blond hair and a good muscular arm for baseball. "But summers are dead. And the rest of the year isn't so great either. There's only about a hundred kids in the combined school, and most of them think I'm weird."

Rose Rita took a fastball from Marta. Marta wasn't half bad, she thought. She had lots of speed, but she needed to work on her accuracy. "So what were you saying about funny weather?" asked Rose Rita innocently, trying to get Marta back to the subject that really interested her.

Marta's mitt smacked as Rose Rita's pitch slammed into it. "Good one. Oh, not weather, I guess, just funny clouds. Funny strange, not funny ha-ha. They look like faces sometimes, or like mythological animals. Know what a chimera is?" She wound up and threw a pretty good curveball, though it broke late and would have been a ball, not a strike.

Rose Rita had borrowed Marta's brother's glove. The ball whapped into it. "Sure," Rose Rita said. "A chimera's one of those mixed-up jigsaw puzzle–type animals. It's part snake and part lion, isn't it?" She wished she knew as much about mythology as Lewis did. She wasn't really sure that she had described a chimera very well.

Marta gave her a superior smile. She had very short bangs, but she kept brushing them back as if they bothered her. "That's kinda the idea of a chimera, but it has three heads. One's a goat's head, one a lion's head, and one a serpent's head. We learned about them in English class last year. Anyhow, one day last week there was a big cloud in the west at sunset. The sun made it all red and purple, and it looked just like the picture of a chimera in my English book. I made Davy look at it. I told him it meant monsters were coming to the Earth, and it scared the bewheekis out of him!" She laughed at the memory. "He can't stand to watch spooky movies or stuff like that."

Rose Rita nodded. Marta had already told her that her little brother's name was Davy, and that he was sort of a scaredy-cat. She glanced down the hill. She could see the general store, and beyond it the dock where her grampa had tied their motorboat. Grampa Galway was spinning yarns with some of the old men who hung out at the store. Rose Rita guessed she had lots of time to find out what Marta knew. "We saw something real odd out on the lake," she said after a couple more pitches. "It was an island that was, like, hidden by this mysterious mist—" Rose Rita broke off. She had an active imagination, and when she started to tell about something, she always had to fight the temptation to turn it into an elaborate story. She shrugged and said, "It was almost like the island just appeared out of nowhere."

"Hey," said Marta, "I've heard about that. It's a few miles to the east of Ivarhaven. Somebody told me that a crazy rich guy from overseas bought a little bitty island after the war and named it Gnomon Island. He had a funny foreign name. Isham? Izman? Something like that."

"Izard?" asked Rose Rita. She was so excited that she flubbed her next throw badly. It hit the ground five feet in front of Marta and took a screwy bounce, but Marta snagged it with some good footwork.

"Izard," she said, straightening up. "That's it! You getting tired? 'Cause we can stop if you want to. It's too hot to play catch anyways."

"Maybe I am a little tired," said Rose Rita. They walked to the swings. The set was like the one Rose Rita remembered from elementary school: a tall A-shaped steel frame. From it dangled eight swings on chains that had rusted almost black. Some were low to the ground for little kids, but two on the end were a comfortable height for Rose Rita and Marta. They chose these two and sat side-by-side. Rose Rita grasped the chains and leaned back. "So why do you think this Izard guy is crazy?"

The grass under the swings had been worn away. Marta looked down as she drew small circles in the dust with the toe of her sneaker. "I dunno. He won't talk much. And he's got this—this servant, I guess you'd call him. Helper. Izard bosses him around like a dog. Anyway, the servant is a little guy, sort of hunchbacked. He's always yellin' at kids, tellin' them the end of the world is comin'. Crazy stuff."

"Huh. Sounds like it's just as well that the two of them don't live in town. I wonder why we had such a hard time seeing Izard's old island," Rose Rita mentioned casually.

Marta's swing creaked as she made it drift back and forth. She wasn't really swinging, just moving around a little. "Who knows? People in town are tellin' lotsa crazy stories about that island too. Like, when the Izard guy bought it after the war, it wasn't much more than a rock. Now there's trees and stuff all over it. People swear that somehow he made it grow. And he built some kinda strange lighthouse. But nobody goes around the place much. The water's not deep enough for the big freighters, and the fish've all gone away from that part of the lake. Besides, like I say, Izard and his helper are mean and no-body wants to hang around them."

"Making the island grow. Making a lighthouse all by himself. Maybe this Izard guy does some kind of magic," suggested Rose Rita carefully.

Marta snorted. "Oh, sure. He just calls on the magic power of pixie dust, an' he can fly to the moon! Anybody who'd think that must have a screw loose or somethin'. He's no magician. They're just in storybooks. Naw, Izard's just a nutty old guy, that's all." Marta began to swing, then stopped with her sneakers skidding on the worn patch. "Talkin' about weird-lookin' clouds, take a gander at that one!"

Rose Rita looked at the patch of sky toward which Marta was pointing. Her stomach felt funny, fluttery and hollow. For a second she didn't think that what she saw could be a cloud at all, but maybe a big helium balloon, like the ones she had seen on TV that were hauled along in the Macy's Thanksgiving Day parade.

But no, it was a wandering white cloud. The edges were puffy, and even as she watched, it began to lose its unusual shape. In the instant that she saw it, the cloud formation had looked just like a circular dial with two hands, one long and one short. A clock face, though of course without numbers. The short hand was almost at twelve, and the long one a little more than fifteen minutes away.

Rose Rita found it hard to get her breath. Lewis had told her that old Isaac Izard did sky magic. He had spent years studying cloud formations and trying to use them to bring about the end of the world. And he had been completely gaga about his magical Doomsday Clock. Had Izard's son, Ishmael, somehow put the clock together? Was the cloud-clock a sign that time was running out? One thing was for sure, Rose Rita knew. She couldn't talk to Marta about such things. Normal people didn't believe in magic!

"I better go," she said, getting up from the swing. "It's getting late, and Grampa'll probably be worrying about me. See ya later."

"Next time you're in town, I'll borrow Davy's bat. We can play some flies an' grounders," Marta called. "I live in the green house over there, the first one on the left past the school. Maybe Davy'll play with us too, if he's not too scared of the clouds!"

"Sure." Rose Rita forced a smile for Marta, then hurried on down the grassy hill. Though the day had been hot and dry, yesterday's rain made the sod squelch under her feet. She trotted toward the general store, feeling a dread she could not quite identify.

Before she had walked all the way across the parking lot, Rose Rita heard an old man's screechy voice coming from inside the store: "Signs and wonders, I tell ye! Look to the sky! Skulls in the clouds, an' devil's heads. The end of days is at hand! And that's not all, neither! Just last week Lem Crawley caught a fish that talked—"

"Oh, come on, Samuel," said the voice of the store owner, Jake Brannigan, just as Rose Rita stepped on the porch. "Would you believe anything Lem told you? After a couple belts of the rotgut he takes out with him when he goes fishing, Lem Crawley starts talking to his bait!"

It was dark inside the store. Peering through the closed screen door, Rose Rita could make out shadowy shapes of men sitting at the checker tables, and two men, the talkers, standing at the counter, one on each side. "The fish spoke to Lem, I tell ye!" insisted the skinny old man who had been warning about signs and wonders. "It said, 'The world will end with the dark of the sun on the fifteenth of August.' Them was its very words! I tell ye, this old world's got a little over two weeks left, and then that's all she wrote!"

Standing with her hand on the screen door, Rose Rita could see a corner of the counter. Jake stood behind it, with a dim lightbulb in a hanging conical metal shade right over his head. He turned around and picked up a paper-covered book from the shelf behind him. "Dark of the sun, huh? Like an eclipse?" He licked his thumb and turned the pages of the book. Finding what he wanted, he peered through his glasses, his lips moving as he read silently. He tossed the book back to the shelf. "Well, the almanac sure don't predict an eclipse for the fifteenth! I guess that trout might have been mistaken. Or maybe it was drinking from the same bottle as Lem!" Everyone laughed, and Rose Rita stepped inside the store to the sound of hoots and guffaws.

"Well," said Grampa Galway, his voice unusually serious. "Here she is, just like I was telling you."

As her eyes adjusted to the dimness of the store, Rose Rita gulped. Turning around and looking at her with a kind of resigned sadness was Jonathan Barnavelt. He shook his head, his red beard wagging.

She had been found out.

CHAPTER TEN

"Can you run this thing?" asked Mrs. Zimmermann, looking doubtfully at the weathered boat.

"There's not much to it," answered Lewis, hoping he was right. "You just fire up the outboard, and use this handle to turn it. If you pull it to the left, the boat goes to the right."

"I hope we can find Ivarhaven Island," said Mrs. Zimmermann. "If we get lost on the lake, we'll be in a real pickle! However, since you can actually *see* Ivarhaven from the shore, I don't suppose we can go too wrong. All right. Let's go see what Rose Rita has been up to!"

It was the first Tuesday in August. The day before, an exasperated Jonathan Barnavelt had called Mrs. Zimmermann to tell her that Rose Rita was on the scene. Mrs. Zimmermann had fretted all night about that, and so she and Lewis had set out before sunrise to make the long drive to the Upper Peninsula. It was late afternoon by the time they had parked Bessie and rented the little motorboat. But even as she stepped into it, Mrs. Zimmermann looked worried.

Lewis was worried too, but it was good to be trusted. He untied the boat, sat down beside the engine, and started it just the way the man had showed him. The outboard motor caught with a *bla-a-att!* and Lewis moved them away from the dock.

It was a calm day, and he did not go very fast. They followed the shoreline to a point where reddish-yellow cliffs rose. Then, ahead and to the left, they could see Ivarhaven, with its white mansion sprawled up the hillside like a set of blocks left behind by an untidy giant. Mrs. Zimmermann, who had clapped a hand onto her head to hold her broad-brimmed floppy hat, made a tutting sound. "Frank Lloyd Wright has a lot to answer for!" she said. "I like a house to look like a house, not a jumble of rectangles and squares. Be careful, Lewis. I'm sure this is deep water."

Lewis didn't answer. He concentrated on guiding their boat across the water. To tell the truth, he didn't feel very well. He had lost lots of sleep, and he had the funny feeling that the boat was moving sideways. The waves caused that, moving from right to left. Behind them the sun was going down, bathing the island in coppery light. As they got closer, Lewis saw the sailboat tied up at the pier, and next to it a fishing boat with its own outboard motor, a little larger than theirs. "That must be the boat that Uncle Jonathan rented," said Lewis, pointing.

"Keep both hands on the tiller!" said Mrs. Zimmermann. "I'm in no mood to be dunked like a doughnut! Careful!"

Lewis throttled the outboard back. They lost speed. Too much, so that he had to give the motor a little juice to get them back on course. Finally they drifted in, and though the bow of their boat clonked against the pier a little hard, it wasn't too bad. Mrs. Zimmermann tied the bowline, and then they stepped up onto the pier, where Lewis tied the stern line off. Trooping down from the house to meet them were Grampa Galway, Uncle Jonathan, and a sheepish-looking Rose Rita.

"Hi, all," Jonathan said, taking Mrs. Zimmermann's suitcase and Lewis's duffel bag. "Well, luckily, Albert says we're welcome to spend a few more days here."

"Got kind of lonesome without anyone around," added Grampa Galway with a grin. "But I didn't know this scamp of a granddaughter of mine had slipped off without letting her friends know."

"I was worried about you, Grampa," said Rose Rita. "Out here all by yourself. What if something happened?"

"And the mystery of the disappearing island had nothing to do with it," put in her grandfather dryly. "Well, well, you're all here now, and I have a pot roast almost ready to eat, so come on in, get settled, and we'll have a regular feast." He led the way back up the path to the house.

It was a good meal, though Lewis could only pick at it. After dinner they played a few hands of cards until Grampa

Galway stretched and yawned. "Guess I'll turn in," he said. "Night."

As soon as the old man had gone to his bedroom, Uncle Jonathan summoned them all into the study. "It's time for a council of war," he said in a serious voice as he shut the door behind him. "Sit down, everybody."

The study had a window seat wide enough for Lewis and Rose Rita to share. Mrs. Zimmermann settled into a big green leather armchair. Uncle Jonathan rolled an office chair with wheels from behind the desk. "Now," he said, putting his hands on his knees, "let's find out what's what. Florence?"

Mrs. Zimmermann told about her research and her communication with good witches in different parts of the world. "Whatever it is," she said hesitantly at last, "it will happen on the fifteenth of this month. It's supposed to be tied in with an eclipse, but there is no eclipse of the sun or moon on that date, so—"

Uncle Jonathan nodded wearily. "Yes, I've heard something about that at this end too. But we know that an eclipse can be staged if you have the right magic."

Lewis, who was feeling light-headed and shaky because he had not been getting much sleep, understood. His uncle could cause a magical eclipse of the moon when the conditions were right. It wasn't like a real eclipse because it could be seen only from a very small area, but during the temporary darkness all sorts of strange and magical things began to happen. "Nobody could eclipse the sun with magic, could they?" he asked anxiously.

Jonathan sighed. "I don't know. My magic wouldn't be nearly strong enough. But someone else who had studied sky magic for years and years—well, that might be a different kettle of fish. Now, Rose Rita. Explain what you're doing here."

Rose Rita's eyes were wide and solemn behind her black-rimmed glasses. "My grampa is pretty old. I worried about him being up here all alone. What if he got hurt on the island and couldn't get to a phone? So I thought I'd come along and—and . . ." Unable to continue, she looked down into her lap.

In a kindly voice Mrs. Zimmermann said, "And snoop around a little bit while you were up here, eh? Well, if you've learned anything, now's the time to spill it!"

"I haven't learned very much," admitted Rose Rita. She told about Marta and her brother and the strange clouds in the sky.

When she had finished speaking, Jonathan tugged thoughtfully at his beard. "There you are. Old Isaac Izard studied cloud formations, hoping to bring the world to an end. His nastier son is conjuring up cloud formations, probably trying to find just the right combination to open the gates to his nefarious magic."

"There's one other thing," said Lewis timidly. He sniffled. "I—I didn't really mean to do it, Mrs. Zimmermann. Honest, I wasn't just snooping around. B-but I found a letter that Professor Athanasius w-wrote to you, and he said I would d-die on the fifteenth of, of this month."

"Oh, dear," said Mrs. Zimmermann. She got out of her chair and patted Lewis on the shoulder. "No wonder you've been losing so much sleep! I should have put that stupid letter in the locked drawer of my desk! Lewis, there must be ways of dealing with evil magic. We have lots and lots of people working on the problem, and I've cast quite a few protective spells over you. The only reason I didn't say anything to you is that, to be honest, I know how much you tend to worry."

"Well," said Jonathan, "now here we are, and here we should stay until this thing is finished. I found a fishing cabin on a point overlooking that blasted island, only it's never in sight. I haven't even seen the shimmering that we first noticed, and I've been puttering around on the water up there for days. My theory, in case you're interested, is that the concealing spell lifts when Ishmael Izard or his assistant, this Clusko, has to go to or leave the island. After one of them passes through, the spell is unstable for a few minutes or a few hours. Those are the times when we could get onto Izard's home territory."

"Clusko," repeated Mrs. Zimmermann. "I wonder if it can be the same man. I knew a Clusko once, Jonathan, and so did you. Remember him? His full name was Ladislav Clusko, and he came poking around New Zebedee a few months after Isaac Izard died."

Jonathan frowned. "That's right! What a memory you have, Florence! I'd been trying to remember where I'd heard that name before. He wanted to put in a bid for Izard's house, but I'd already bought it by then." He turned to Lewis. "You see, Lewis, old Isaac had avoided paying the taxes on his place for years. He thought he'd end the world and not have to worry about it, I suppose.

Anyway, when he died, the place was sold to settle the taxes, and I made the high bid. Ladislav Clusko came to town about three weeks too late. It might be the same man, Florence. I don't know if I'd even recognize him if I saw him, though. I met him only once, for about ten minutes, and that was years and years ago."

"He turned up again," said Mrs. Zimmermann. "According to what I have learned, he tried to put together a group of evil magicians in Europe about five years ago. There was some kind of magical duel on Walpurgis Night in the Hartz Mountains, and his little gang scattered to the winds. I have the feeling it must be the same man, but why or how he hooked up with Ishmael Izard, I couldn't even guess."

Jonathan stood up and began to pace. "Well, we know that Mr. Clusko visits the general store about twice a week for ice and groceries. Now that we've got enough of us here to split up and watch the store as well as the place where that weird island is supposed to be, maybe we can finally get a lead. Florence, there's an Army surplus store over in Marquette. I'll drive there first thing in the morning and see if I can pick up some walkie-talkies. The main thing for us to do is to find a way back to this Gnome Island, or whatever it's called."

That night Lewis went to bed in the same room he had used on their visit in June. He wasn't very sleepy, and he took a book to bed with him. It was *A Guide to the Upper Peninsula*, which he had found in the study, a tall, thin book crammed with color photos of wildlife and landscapes. Lewis turned the pages, staring at the colorful Painted Cliffs, at snow-covered winter forests, at lakes and hills and waterfalls. He began to yawn.

He found a photo of the woods near Porcupine Bay in the autumn. Maples and birches and smoke trees blazed in yellows, oranges, and scarlets. The camera gazed through the trunks, which receded into the distance. Tangles of undergrowth ran through the photo. It was a peaceful scene. Lewis was about to turn the page when something caught his eye. It was a patch of white away in the distance, half hidden by two slender tree trunks.

Lewis idly wondered what it was. An animal of some kind? But it was too big to be a rabbit or anything like that. He yawned again, closing his eyes for a moment.

Then he glanced back at the page. The white thing had moved. He was sure of it. Now it peeked from behind a tree that was a bit closer. Lewis stared at it until his eyes ached. He had the frightening feeling that he had fallen into the photograph. He wanted to tear his gaze away, but he found that he couldn't do it.

His eyes burned from strain. They watered, and the white shape became wavery. It moved! Or was that a trick of his tired eyes? Had it flopped from one tree to the next with a horrible, broken-limbed lurching movement? Lewis was almost sure it had!

He wanted to slip out of bed and yell for help, but he felt paralyzed. The flopping, flapping thing was coming closer. He wanted to see what it was, though he dreaded the very thought of what it might look like. Maybe if he stared very hard—

Lewis had a sudden uncanny sense that something was wrong. He forced his eyes off the book. Across the room from the foot of his bed was a tall window looking out over the lake. Beneath the window was a pool of shadow, unreachable by the light from Lewis's reading lamp. Faintly glowing in the darkness were two spots of yellowish light, as round as eggs. They did not move. Lewis reached a trembling hand out to his lamp. It had a slim base, like a candlestick. He grabbed it, and with a sudden movement he held it high, flooding the dark recess below the window and between the curtains with light.

A shaggy dark thing hissed, leaped, and climbed the wall! It was the night creature from the engraving of King Solomon! Lewis screamed, a dry, thin, high screech as the monstrous form swarmed up the wall, then across the ceiling, clinging like some loathsome fly, its round head twisting on a spindly neck so the yellow eyes were always fixed on him—

Something ice-cold touched his hand!

Lewis looked down. The book had fallen to the bed and was cracked open. And from the crack a skeletal hand had reached out, clenching, trying to grab his own hand—

With a convulsive movement, Lewis dropped the lamp and kicked the book from the bed. He ran to the door and threw it open—

Facing him was something in the shape of a woman. Her face was like a skull, with a fiery light blazing in the hollow eye sockets. And from the creature came a piercing wail, a rising and falling cry that froze the blood in

Lewis's veins. From beyond the apparition he heard Mrs. Zimmermann's voice: "Lewis! What in heaven's name is wrong?"

With another shriek, Lewis threw himself at the ghostly figure. For a second he felt as if he were passing through a cold mist. Then he was falling into Mrs. Zimmermann's arms and was babbling out the story of what had happened.

CHAPTER ELEVEN

"A banshee," said Uncle Jonathan. "Another of friend Izard's little calling cards. He seems to be telling us that he has traveled all over the world and can summon spirits from all kinds of belief, from Japan to Ireland."

It was morning, and Lewis was feeling less terrified, though he still wondered if he were losing his mind. "Was it real?" he asked.

Jonathan looked at Mrs. Zimmermann. "Let's ask the expert. Florence?"

Mrs. Zimmermann shook her head and prodded an untidy strand of hair back into place. "I think not. Lewis, I think these things, the banshee and the *Kuchisake Onna*, are like your uncle's illusions. They look and even feel real, but they exist only in your mind. I think old creepy Izard is just trying to keep you terrified by sending these things. The more off balance you are, the harder it is for you to fight back."

Rose Rita said, "So why don't we fight back? Couldn't you blast him with a purple lightning bolt or something? I don't like sitting around while he does this spooky stuff to my friends!"

Mrs. Zimmermann smiled. "Because we are not evil wizards," she said. "That's the short answer. It's one thing to use magic in self-defense. It's another to go around looking for people to zap. Besides, from what we have learned already, we know that Izard has quite a few wizardly friends in his plot. We can't afford to take a chance in attacking him until, first, we know exactly what he's up to and, second, we can find him. But don't worry. We're working on it."

That day both Mrs. Zimmermann and Uncle Jonathan left Ivarhaven Island. Despite Rose Rita's pleas, she and Lewis had to stay behind. They stood watching the motorboat skim toward Porcupine Bay, and Rose Rita flopped down to sit on a rock with her chin in her hands. "It's not fair," she complained. "Somebody needs to look after them. They're not as young as they used to be."

"But it might be dangerous," objected Lewis. He immediately wished he hadn't said that. It made him sound like the world's biggest chicken.

Rose Rita's eyes snapped. "That's exactly why we should be with them! Look, Lewis, we've got to make a pact."

"Why?" asked Lewis.

Patiently Rose Rita said, "We've got to agree that we

can't let Mrs. Zimmermann run around without one of us along."

"But she's a sorceress," Lewis pointed out. "And she wouldn't like us poking our noses into her business."

"She's my friend," shot back Rose Rita. "I won't have her getting into trouble all by herself. The next time Mrs. Zimmermann gets ready to go off on some kind of expedition, one of us has to go. Even if we have to sneak to do it!"

She was staring at Lewis so hard that he didn't have the heart to disagree. So he said, "Okay," although he didn't feel very brave or even comfortable with the idea. All the rest of the day Lewis was jumpy and fearful. Then, as the sun sank low in the west, he heard the putter of an outboard motor. He and Rose Rita hurried down to the dock once more. To his surprise Lewis saw the boat that his uncle had rented moving across the water with three passengers inside. His heart pounded. The third passenger was Clusko, huddled in the bow and looking angry.

As soon as the boat was tied, Uncle Jonathan stepped onto the pier. He was holding a heavy paper bag in the crook of his left arm. With his right hand he helped Clusko out, and then Mrs. Zimmermann. "You'd never have beaten me," whined Clusko, "if I had my full power!"

Rose Rita looked from him to Mrs. Zimmermann. "Zap?" she asked.

"Zap," replied Mrs. Zimmermann firmly. "This man saw me in town and tried to cast a spell on me. I felt the magic building and turned it away just in time. It wasn't very strong, and I don't think he has enough moxie really to hurt me, but I counteracted his spell. Then I hit him back with a whammy that makes him have to do my bidding, at least until sunset. Let's go to the house, Mr. Clusko. March!"

Like a puppet worked by strings, Clusko did march in a jerky, lurching way toward the house. He was silent in the presence of Grampa Galway when Jonathan explained that they were going to ask him a few questions about the islands. "I'll start dinner, then," Grampa Galway said. He went inside.

"It's a warm afternoon," Mrs. Zimmermann said. "Let's stay out here for a few minutes. All right, Mr. Clusko. You are going to answer Jonathan Barnavelt's questions truthfully. Understand?"

The small man nodded, though his face writhed in an expression of hatred. Lewis looked at Rose Rita, who was staring at Mrs. Zimmermann with wide eyes. He knew what she was thinking. Mrs. Zimmermann was never harsh. But now her voice was as cold and as hard as iron.

"How do we get to Gnomon Island?" Jonathan asked.

Clusko wriggled uncomfortably. "No," he said. "Nn-nn-ooo. . . ." Then his lips twitched. He spat out each word unwillingly: "It . . . is a spell . . . of revealing. It is in the Key of Solomon. B-but there are wards. He will know if you use the spell."

Uncle Jonathan leaned closer. "Then how can we get to the island without his knowing?"

Clusko closed his eyes. "Please. Please. He will do terrible things to me. . . . You . . . must wait until he passes through the barrier, to the island or away from it, and move quickly . . . I feel his mind! No! No, master! Help me! He knows I'm here!"

The last words came out as a desperate groan. Lewis winced. He almost felt sorry for this frightened little man.

Jonathan said, "Help us and we will protect you. Now, here's the sixty-four dollar question: What do you know about the Doomsday Clock?"

Lewis was astonished at the change in Clusko's face. It turned red, then white. The man's eyes rolled, and his mouth quivered as if he were trying to clamp it shut. "Time is running out!" he shouted, spitting flecks of white foam. "When the clock counts noon on the fifteenth, a Day of Darkness will begin! Fire will consume all the unworthy, and only his followers will remain to inherit the earth—no, master! I didn't mean to tell them! I won't—I won't—help me!"

Rose Rita jumped in alarm. Lewis cried out. Something had seized Clusko, something that Lewis could not see. It jerked the little man this way and that, and then rose into the air with him. He dangled like a mouse caught in the clutches of a hawk. Against the crimson sky a huge dim shapeless shadow fluttered and flapped. Clusko gibbered and screamed, his voice thin. Mrs. Zimmermann spoke a spell and raised her umbrella. Purple light flared, and for a second Lewis saw the outline of something like a vast dark bird with outspread wings.

Suddenly Clusko's flesh bubbled as if tiny creatures lived inside and were trying to burst out. His eyes swelled and drifted apart, and a dark hole gaped open where his nose used to be. Human flesh became green scales, and claws grew out of his shrinking limbs.

The force that had seized Clusko shook him and threw him aside. Clusko's body flew through the air and hit the rocks with a squelch. The misshapen thing that had once been human bawled in a terrible animal way. Claws clicked on the rocks as the thing scuttled into the dark water of the lake. Then it was gone.

Lewis heard Rose Rita gasping and sobbing. Mrs. Zimmermann had her arm around Rose Rita's shoulders. "Our friend Mr. Izard doesn't like it when his slaves turn on him," she said grimly. "I should have seen that coming."

From the house Grampa Galway called, "So six of us for dinner, then?"

With a sick look on his face Jonathan yelled back, "Just five. Mr. Clusko didn't stay."

The next day Uncle Jonathan and Mrs. Zimmermann tried out the walkie-talkies that Jonathan had bought at the Army surplus store. Mrs. Zimmermann also took Lewis aside. "I have something for you," she said. "First, take the slip of parchment from your wallet. Do it very carefully."

Lewis began to breathe hard. He removed the piece of parchment, hating its strange texture and the way it seemed to wriggle in his grasp as if it were alive.

Mrs. Zimmermann held out a small book, barely three by five inches. It had a badly scuffed blue cover, and the edges of its pages were yellow with age. "Here," she said. "Put the parchment between two leaves toward the middle."

Lewis opened the book at random. It was written in some foreign language, with English translations between the lines. At the top of the page was the heading "La Vega's Tagalog/English Maritime Phrasebook." Lewis saw that the English sentences on the page said things like "When, pray, is the next spring tide?" and "I require a pilot to assist my vessel." Quickly, though, he put the parchment in the book and then closed the covers. Mrs. Zimmermann handed him a thick rubber band. "Now snap this around it, just for insurance," she said. "You don't want to let that parchment get away from you."

When he had finished, Lewis asked, "Is this some sort of magic?"

Mrs. Zimmermann winked. "It could be. You could think of this old book, which I bought for a quarter at a junk store, as having all my most powerful magic spells in it, written in code. You could say that I'd be helpless without it, magically speaking. Just imagine that it contains a powerful spell that could even destroy a magical clock."

Lewis felt confused. Was Mrs. Zimmermann telling him that this actually *was* a book of magic? He had never known her to use one before. Her magic was all done with amulets and spoken spells and her umbrella-staff. But, following Mrs. Zimmermann's advice, he put the book in his hip pocket. "Now what?" he asked.

"Now comes the hardest part," replied Mrs. Zimmermann in a solemn voice. "We wait."

Days passed. Lewis grew more and more troubled. The twelfth arrived. Then the thirteenth. He had only two days left! Perhaps the whole world did! That night he lay awake fretting and worrying. That was why he heard the voices.

His uncle had said that he was going to scout around, and he had left for his fishing cabin that afternoon. But Lewis heard him speaking and guessed he must have returned. Lewis slipped out of bed, threw on his clothes, and went down the hall. The voices were coming from Mrs. Zimmermann's room, and once he was close enough, Lewis realized that his uncle wasn't there. He was speaking to Mrs. Zimmermann on the walkie-talkie.

"He's just left," his uncle was saying. "If my blasted outboard hadn't gone on the fritz—listen, Florence, go fire up your boat and get to the point as quickly as you can. He'll be there in half an hour. The barrier will be down as he passes through, and you can enter. It's our only hope!"

"I'm on my way," said Mrs. Zimmermann. She began to move around in her room, probably getting dressed.

Lewis gulped. He and Rose Rita had made a pact that one of them had to go along on expeditions like this. He knew that Mrs. Zimmermann was going to try to follow Ishmael Izard right onto Gnomon Island.

He reached a decision. He would have to go with Mrs. Zimmermann. He couldn't very well wake Rose Rita and beg *her* to go! Though he was scared to death, the look of contempt he would be sure to get from Rose Rita if he failed bothered him more than his fear. Moving as softly as he could, Lewis ran outside and darted down to the dock.

Where could he hide? He clambered into the rented boat. Right up forward was a little compartment for life jackets, fishing tackle, and such. It had a sliding door that Lewis yanked open. He crept inside, turned, and pulled the door closed again. The fit wasn't comfortable. He sat with his knees drawn up to his chin, the top of his head touching the deck. But he was hidden, at least.

After what seemed like a long time he felt the boat rock. Then the engine sputtered to life, and the boat was moving. Lewis tried not to rattle around as the bow rose and dipped. He held on tight to a life-jacket rack beside him. Minutes passed. Then Mrs. Zimmermann cut the engine, and for a time they just drifted.

The forward compartment smelled of old bait and fish, and soon felt as muggy as a steam bath. A sweaty Lewis strained for any sound. Finally he caught a whine almost as thin as a mosquito's buzz. It was another boat. He could tell that it passed by. And then he heard the splash as Mrs. Zimmermann started to row. He felt a cold, electric tingle all over. He had felt that before, when they passed through the barrier around Gnomon Island.

Lewis realized that something terrible could happen at any moment.

Their boat was taking them straight into the clutches of a powerful and crazed magician.

CHAPTER TWELVE

The sun was just coming up as Rose Rita heard the boat approaching Ivarhaven Island. She ran to the docks. As soon as Jonathan Barnavelt came close enough, she yelled, "Mrs. Zimmermann's gone! And Lewis too!"

Jonathan looked up sharply. "What! Lewis?"

"It's my fault," confessed Rose Rita. Hurriedly she explained how she and Lewis had worried and how they had pledged to follow if Mrs. Zimmermann tried to slip away on her own. "I'm worried sick," she finished.

"I'll go after them," said Jonathan.

"Me too."

Jonathan gave her a long look. "Okay, but let your grampa know—"

"He knows."

Rose Rita jumped a mile. Grampa Galway had been

walking down the path from the house to the dock, and now he was right behind her. He put a hand on her shoulder. "Your old granddad isn't stupid," he said softly. "Jonathan, for some time now I've suspected that you had more up your sleeve than parlor-magic tricks. And I've always known there was something, well, different about Florence Zimmermann. I think it's probably just as well that I don't know exactly what's up, but I do know that you have some serious business to attend to. Watch after my granddaughter."

"I will, Albert," said Jonathan. "Climb in, Rose Rita! Time's a-wasting!"

Rose Rita waved good-bye to her grandfather as they roared away from Ivarhaven Island. She felt anxious. Would she ever see him alive again?

Would she ever see *anyone* alive again?

It was the fourteenth of August.

Could it be the world's last day?

From the moment he had set foot on Gnomon Island, Lewis had felt strange. He had waited in the cramped compartment of the boat until Mrs. Zimmermann left the boat. Then he had crawled out and followed her. The night was dark, with no moon, and Lewis quickly became lost.

To his surprise the sky began to lighten. More time had passed than he had thought. As the sun rose, he found that he was wandering in a tangle of fir trees. He climbed the slope until he reached the edge of the lawn in front of the dark tower. From there he could see that the sky was red in the east. Overhead, clouds that twisted and formed into terrible likenesses of screaming faces and clutching hands were gathering.

Lewis found the pathway that led down through the trees and followed it. Soon the little cottage came into view. Through the single window Lewis caught a flash of purple. Mrs. Zimmermann! Relief washed over him in a soothing wave. But then, in the next second, fear clamped a cold fist on Lewis's heart.

He heard a sneering voice say, "You were foolish to come. You can do nothing! Not without this!"

Mrs. Zimmermann's voice replied, "That's what you think, Ishmael Izard. You have studied magic. You should know that a sorcerer can store great power in a grimoire. Well, it so happens that *I* have entrusted a book to a good friend of mine. A book with something very special in it that can take care of you and your insane plans."

The man laughed. "So you've given a book of spells to that bumbling, red-bearded, potbellied fool who bought my father's house! He will be very easy to deal with. I can take your grimoire away from him as easily as I took your stupid umbrella away from you! Now what to do with you? I don't want to kill you, because after the world has changed, I will need servants. I know! I have just the spot. You will have a ringside seat at the end of the world! Come along with me—I command it!"

Lewis shrank around the corner of the house. Crouching low, he saw a tall man with long gray hair step out of the cottage. He wore a black suit and a black turtleneck shirt. With bony arms he made mystic gestures, and in obedience to them, Mrs. Zimmermann walked out of the house. Her white hair straggled loose from its bun. She wore one of her purple dresses and her black sensible walking shoes. With her back straight, she strode up the path. Izard's expression was cruel and triumphant as he marched her toward the tower. Soon they were out of sight.

Lewis hurried to the front. The cottage door was open. He went inside and looked wildly around. Then he saw what he was looking for. Someone had stuck Mrs. Zimmermann's black umbrella, its crystal globe gleaming dully, up in the rafters. It was far out of Lewis's reach. He looked for something to climb on—and then he heard the crunch of footsteps outside! Without hesitating, Lewis dived under one of the beds in the room. He pressed against the wall, hoping that no one could see him. It was dusty under there, and his nose itched, making him want to sneeze. Lewis squeezed his nostrils shut with his fingers, fighting the feeling. He glimpsed Izard's feet. He heard the man chuckle. "So much for the real wizard," the man growled to himself. "Now to lay the trap for the fool!"

Lewis realized that Izard was talking about his uncle. He was so frightened that he thought he would lose his mind.

"We have to get more gas," said Jonathan Barnavelt. "I've got some at the fishing cabin."

Rose Rita was beginning to feel panic. It was almost sunset. For several hours she and Jonathan had been zigging and zagging across the surface of the lake, trying to catch sight of Gnomon Island. Jonathan had used the walkie-talkie time and time again, but he had failed to make contact with Mrs. Zimmermann.

Jonathan guided the boat to shore, then hurried up the hillside to a log cabin. He soon came back, carrying a red gas can. He glugged gasoline into the outboard motor tank. Rose Rita wrinkled her nose at the sharp smell. "Okay," he said. "Let's try again."

Before long they were back on Lake Superior. Rose Rita kept looking uneasily toward the west. The sun was getting low, and she knew that if they didn't find some trace soon, they would have to head back to Ivarhaven Island. She wondered if they were even on the right track. Jonathan seemed convinced that Mrs. Zimmermann had headed for Gnomon Island, but maybe she had come up with a different plan. She might be anywhere—

"There it is," said Jonathan suddenly.

Rose Rita saw the ripply waves of air. Jonathan turned the nose of the boat and gunned the engine. "It's going away!" she yelled as the ripples began to fade.

"Hang on!" roared Jonathan.

Rose Rita grabbed hold of the boat's side with a tight grip. The craft almost leaped out of the water as Jonathan gave it the gas. Bouncing on her seat, Rose Rita thought this was the way a skimmed stone might feel as it went skipping over water—slap! Slap! Slap!

They reached the barrier and zoomed through it, and suddenly the eastern side of Gnomon Island reared dead ahead. The tower with its flying-buttress stair was jet-black against the crimson sky. Jonathan turned, cut back on the gas, and they followed the shoreline to the left until they came to the inlet and the pier. "They're here," Rose Rita said, pointing to the dock. Mrs. Zimmermann's rented motorboat was tied there. It was the only one.

"And it looks as if Sneaky Pete is away," Jonathan declared. "That's just peachy keen, as far as I'm concerned." He grabbed the walkie-talkie and said into it, "Florence! Are you there? I'm about to dock at Gnomon Island." He switched to "listen," but all Rose Rita could hear from the little speaker was a crackle of static.

They secured the boat and climbed onto the dock. Rose Rita looked up the winding pathway with doubt in her heart. It would be dark very soon. And then what? She could only hope that Mrs. Zimmermann and Lewis were all right.

When night fell, Lewis was still hiding. He had crawled out from under the bed as soon as Izard left. At the doorway he caught a glimpse of the man striding down the path toward the dock, and a few minutes later he had heard the sound of a motorboat moving away. Immediately Lewis had run to the dark tower. Mrs. Zimmermann was nowhere to be found. He yelled her name, and only faint echoes of his own voice answered.

Lewis spent the day roaming the island, trying to find some hiding place where Mrs. Zimmermann might be locked away. No luck. He got hungry enough to return to the cabin in the afternoon, where he opened a can of beans and ate them cold. Then he hid the can. He found a stack of spare Army blankets on a shelf in the cottage, and he took one. He went down to the dock and looked through Mrs. Zimmermann's boat for some weapon he might use, but he found nothing. Then, when he heard the distant drone of a returning motorboat, Lewis fled into the woods. He found a place where some fallen branches had made a sort of cave. Creeping into this, Lewis rolled up in the blanket. He was close enough to the path that ran to the tower to see anyone passing by. His plan was just to wait and watch, but minutes passed, and then hours. Sometime around sunset he fell asleep, exhausted by fear and by the long day he had spent.

He dreamed of hairy, creeping things. . . .

CHAPTER THIRTEEN

Jonathan and Rose Rita explored Izard's cabin without finding any trace of him or Mrs. Zimmermann. Then, in the falling dusk, they climbed up to the tower and scouted around there. Still no luck. Jonathan took a deep breath. "I can think of one place they might be," he said. "But it's not somewhere you can go, Rose Rita. Too dangerous. You wait here."

Rose Rita watched Jonathan walk to the base of the strange leaning stairs up to the top of the tower. He hesitated, then began to climb. Rose Rita grew dizzy just watching him. The steps were high, and walking up them looked awkward. The light was fading now, so Rose Rita could see the tower, the steps, and Jonathan only in silhouette.

After what felt like an hour Jonathan reached the top of

the tower and stepped onto a sort of round platform that ran around it. "There's a door," he called down in a voice made thin by distance.

"Be careful!" shouted Rose Rita.

She heard the faint click of the door opening, then a slam. And then nothing. Rose Rita counted to a hundred. Then she started toward the base of the stairs. But a sound stopped her short. It was the distant sound of an outboard motor. Suddenly all was quiet. Immediately Rose Rita dashed to the base of the tower. She hid behind it as someone approached. Peeking around she could just make out a figure in the dusk. It was a tall thin man dressed entirely in black. He stood at the bottom of the stairs and clapped his hands together. "So the fly has come to the spider," he said softly. "Now my revenge will be complete!" And he *ran* up the unrailed stairs, taking them two at a time.

At the top he knocked on the door. "Comfortable, Jonathan Barnavelt? Enjoying your visit, Florence Zimmermann?" he called in a sneering voice. "By now you have discovered that the door cannot be opened from the inside—not without a word of power that only I know. But to make doubly sure, I will cast a nice little paralyzing spell on the two of you!" He chanted in some foreign language, and Rose Rita heard the door open and close again.

Rose Rita ran down the path toward the boats. But before she had reached the clearing and the cottage, she stopped. Izard had mentioned Jonathan and Mrs. Zimmermann, but not Lewis. Did that mean that Lewis was still free? Was he a captive somewhere else on the island? Or had something awful happened to him?

She hesitated so long that she heard footsteps approaching. Rose Rita left the path and, in the darkness, blundered into the woods. She crouched as Ishmael Izard passed by, grumbling to himself. "No book of spells! What could the witch have done with it? No matter, no matter, they're harmless now, and after noon tomorrow they will have no power. I'll—"

Rose Rita backed away from the path and stepped on something soft. "My hand!" yelped Lewis.

He came surging up out of his hiding place as Rose Rita stumbled and fell.

"Who's there?" barked Izard.

Rose Rita heard Lewis's frantic attempt to run, and she heard him hit the ground hard. "Help!" he shouted.

"Got you!" yelled Izard. "Who's this, who's this? The nephew of that miserable Barnavelt! Well, well, you have until tomorrow before they come for you, after all. You might as well spend your last night with me! Maybe you can tell me something I need to know!"

Rose Rita heard Lewis whimpering, then the sounds of footsteps on the path. She got to her knees. Feeling around in the dark, she found a rough blanket. Then she pushed through the underbrush, hoping she was heading toward the path. A twig lashed across her face, stinging her cheek. She almost lost her glasses. But finally she came onto open ground. She had to grope her way downhill. At last she saw a yellow rectangle of light, the single window in Izard's cabin. Dropping to all fours, she sneaked up to the wall. The window was open about six inches or so. Through it she could hear Izard's voice: "I am weary now. Lie on that bunk. Lie on it! You will sleep. I will let you sleep until your last hour has come. And then I will watch your sufferings! Sleep now. I command it. Sleep. . . ."

To her horror Rose Rita felt her eyelids droop. She backed away from that hypnotic voice. Too late! She barely had time to creep to the side of the cabin before sleep overcame her and she fell into unconsciousness.

For Lewis it was as if he had fallen into a bottomless pit. One moment he lay on the cot, struggling, and the next he was dead asleep. And then, somehow, he was awake again. A ray of daylight came through the window. Lewis raised himself up and became aware that Ishmael Izard was standing in front of him, arms folded. "Your time is almost up, boy," purred the evil magician. "It is the fifteenth, and the appointed hour of your passing! But you have one hope for my mercy. I gave you the runes, and no doubt they have since vanished. They have a way of doing that, you know! IIe who holds the runes is powerless against the forces of shadow. But I am a magician. I could hold back your doom. I could let you live."

"Wh-what?" asked Lewis. "Where's Mrs. Zimmermann?"

Izard laughed. "I will take you to see her, if you cooperate. Yes, and let you stay with her and with your foolish uncle while the world is cleansed of all but my followers. On this island, and here alone, will you be safe from the coming destruction. But your life is draining away, as sands trickle through an hourglass! Tell me, if you know—where is the witch's book?"

Lewis became uncomfortably aware of the weight in his jeans pocket. "Wh-what book?" he asked.

"A book of spells, she said," returned Izard. "It is my only minor worry. A trifle. I thought your uncle had it, but he did not. You have one chance. Tell me where the book is—or I let you die among the shadows!"

The light in the cabin began to flicker. Lewis cast a fearful gaze at the window. The daylight was fluttering, as if the wings of some creature were blotting it out. "The book!" yelled Izard. "Fool of a boy! Do you think Mrs. Zimmermann would rather see you die? Your last chance!"

Lewis couldn't fight the overwhelming fear. Now bits of shadow were flittering through the screen, through the slightly opened window. They were no larger than moths, fragments of darkness that swirled in the air, that moved toward him. "Here!" he screamed, yanking the little volume from his pocket. "Here it is!"

Izard raised his right hand, and the shadowy forms flowed back through the window. "Very well, boy," he said calmly. He opened the door. "We will walk to the tower together. Come with me."

Lewis felt his legs moving. It was as if he could not control them. He stood and followed Izard to the pathway. It was a clouded day, with winks of sunlight appearing and disappearing through strange, swollen, rolling clouds. From the height of the sun it seemed like very late morning, almost noon, in fact. Lewis still had the little book clutched in his hand.

"You must give me the witch's spell book," Izard said. "I will not force you. You have to do it of your own will. But if you do not, then I will let the spell work itself out. You will die. The book, if you please."

And then, for the first time, Lewis remembered that the slip of parchment was inside the book. He held the volume out. Izard took it from him with an air of triumph. He opened it and looked down. Then he glanced sharply up again. "What trick is this?" he snarled. "This is not—"

Something white fluttered from between the pages of the dictionary. "You took the runes back," said Lewis.

Izard's face jerked in terror. "Fool!" he shrieked. "You will take it back!" He grabbed for the parchment, but it blew from his grasp. He ran to chase it—

And Rose Rita barrel-rolled from beneath a bush, tripping him! The parchment soared away, over the trees. Lewis backed away. "Look out!" he screamed to Rose Rita.

The air was full of those whirling shadows again. Izard rose to his knees. He screamed. With madness in his eyes he turned toward Lewis. "Stop them!" he yelled. "Without me the world will end and there will be no master to rebuild it! The Doomsday Clock is running! Stop—"

The shadows closed in. They covered Izard like a ragged cloak. He fought his way to his feet and lunged toward Lewis. His clawing hands emerged from the darkness, but they had become transparent, like shadows themselves. "Stop them!" wailed the magician in a muffled, moaning voice. Then, with a horrible tearing sound, the shadows pulled apart. They left nothing behind. They spun like a whirlwind, from which Izard's awful howls of anguish spilled. Then they rose into the air, higher and higher.

"Quick," Rose Rita said, grabbing Lewis's arm. "We've got to save your uncle and Mrs. Zimmermann!"

Something fell to the path in front of them with a plop. It was what remained of the dictionary. The pages smoked, charred, and, one by one, blew away on the rising wind.

CHAPTER FOURTEEN

Lewis had no time to feel sick at the terrible fate that had overtaken Ishmael Izard. "You heard him! The clock is still ticking!" shouted Rose Rita. "We've got to find it and shut it off!"

"B-but we're safe here on the island," objected Lewis. "H-he said so!"

Rose Rita gave him a fierce look. "Sure, *we* may be safe. But what about Grampa Galway? What about Mom and Dad? What about every friend of ours in the world? If we don't stop this thing, they'll all be fried!"

Lewis knew she was right. "But where is everyone?" he asked.

"I know where they are. Follow me!" snapped Rose Rita.

They ran up the zigzagging path to the dark tower.

The sky overhead roiled with ragged black clouds. They left an opening, almost like a tunnel, for the sun, but its pale light only seemed to make the clouds more threatening. Lewis had a feeling that all around him the shadows were lurching and twitching, reaching out for the world. Under the trees dark pools shifted and surged, as if greedy to devour the light.

Rose Rita and Lewis burst out at the base of the narrow stairs that led up to the top of the tower. "I'll go," volunteered Rose Rita. "I'm not as afraid of heights as—"

"We'll *both* go," returned Lewis firmly. "You're not gonna leave me alone down here!"

Rose Rita nodded and led the way. Before he had gone a dozen steps, Lewis felt his knees begin to shake. The stairs were very narrow and very steep. A wrong step, and he'd plunge over the side. Why hadn't Izard created a railing? But as soon as he wondered that, Lewis knew the answer: The evil wizard had planned that only his enemies would ever make the journey up the stairs.

Halfway to the top Lewis felt his head spinning. He dropped to all fours and crept upward. "Go ahead," he gasped. "I'm coming as fast as I can."

"Don't look down," advised Rose Rita. She hurried upward, her steps firm. Lewis was only three quarters of the way to the top when Rose Rita reached the sealed door. "I'm going to try to open this!" she roared. "You pull while I push!"

Lewis heard his uncle yell something in reply. He forced himself up, fighting the terrible feeling of nausea in the pit of his stomach. Step by step he crawled until finally he reached the platform where Rose Rita stood. It was wider than the stairs. In fact, it ran all the way around the top of the tower. Lewis dragged himself to his feet. "C-can I help?"

Rose Rita grunted. "Your uncle said some sort of magic spell, and I heard the door go 'ping,' but it didn't open. This crazy latch is on some kind of strong spring. When I turn it, I can't push, and when I push, I can't turn it. I'll try to open the latch. When I tell you, shove the door as hard as you can!"

"O-okay," said Lewis. He hated to think of what would happen if he bounced off the door and took two steps back. They would be the last steps he would ever take. All around the top of the tower the clouds were swirling now, and the sun was almost directly overhead. They had only minutes left.

Rose Rita gripped the thick iron handle and twisted it with all her might. "Now!" she said through clenched teeth. "Hard!"

Lewis closed his eyes. He hurled himself at the door. His shoulder thudded against it—and the door swung open with a groan! Shouting in alarm, Lewis tumbled into a small round room. It held only two straight chairs, back to back. Uncle Jonathan and Mrs. Zimmermann were in the chairs, bound hand and foot.

"Attaboy, Lewis!" yelled Uncle Jonathan, who was facing the door. "Use your Scout knife and get us loose!"

"Hurry," urged Mrs. Zimmermann. "We don't have much time left."

Rose Rita was holding the door open. She kicked off

her sneakers. "This thing doesn't have a doorknob inside," she said. "I'll jam it open with my shoes. Help your uncle, Lewis. I'll untie Mrs. Zimmermann."

"Careful," said Mrs. Zimmermann. "It's wizard-rope. Tug the wrong way on a knot, and it'll grab you!"

Lewis took his Boy Scout knife from his jeans pocket. He opened the blade and said, "Where should I cut?"

"Anywhere!" ordered Jonathan. "This is just regular clothesline! I don't rate a special wrapping like Haggy Face here!"

Lewis sawed through a loop of the rope, then another. Jonathan tugged his arm free, then took the knife from Lewis and cut through the line on his left arm and his legs. He sprang up and said, "Stand back, Rose Rita. I'm pretty good with magic knots!"

He made some passes over the knots binding Mrs. Zimmermann's right arm. They squirmed, then suddenly untied themselves. In a tone of relief Mrs. Zimmermann said, "Thank heavens! I'll take it from here." She made a gesture of her own, and then she pulled herself up, the rope first stretching like taffy, then dissolving into puffs of mist. "We've got to get my umbrella," she said. "Old Droopy Drawers left it in the rafters of his cottage. Where is he?"

Lewis swallowed hard. "Th-the s-shadows got him," he said. "I g-gave him the parchment with the b-book, and he took back the runes."

"Good riddance," she said gruffly. "Let's go!"

"I'm with you!" declared Jonathan, picking up his crystal-headed cane from under his chair. "Follow me, everyone!"

Lewis had thought climbing up the steps was hard. Going down was worse. Though no wind stirred, the clouds were rushing in a circle overhead, and the movement made Lewis feel as if he were pitching sideways. But with his uncle's hand firmly on his shoulder, he forced himself to take one step after another until at last he reached the ground again.

"I'll get my staff!" barked Mrs. Zimmermann. "You see if you can find this blasted clock! It's only five minutes before noon!"

"I'll go with you," said Rose Rita, who had paused to tug her sneakers back on. She and Mrs. Zimmermann dashed down the pathway to the cottage.

Jonathan leaned against the tower, pressing his ear to the stones. "I can't hear a blessed thing," he groused, waving his cane wildly. "What did Izard do? Make a magical electric Doomsday Clock? That wasn't his style!"

Lewis looked up the steep hill. All around the edge of it was darkness. The grass itself and all the weird sculptures were in the faint sunlight that streamed through the hole in the clouds. The shadows were blurred, and Lewis had the sick feeling that the sun itself was fading out.

Then he noticed something. The sculpture closest to the tower was a set of spears pointing upward from a concrete dome. One was in the center, surrounded by a circle of three, and a final circle of eight spears surrounded them. Lewis suddenly realized there were exactly a dozen. Except now that he looked at them, they looked less like spears and more like the hands of a gigantic clock. Could that be the answer? Twelve clock hands, twelve hours, twelve noon? His head spun. The answer seemed so close, and yet it slipped through his mind. He could no more hold on to it than he could pick up a handful of water.

Uncle Jonathan pointed toward the path. "Here come Florence and Rose Rita. Maybe they'll have a bright idea."

Lewis looked back. Mrs. Zimmermann had called upon her powers. The umbrella had become a tall ebony wand, a brilliant purple crystal at its tip throbbing and shooting out rays of light. Mrs. Zimmermann's purple dress had become a billowing black robe with purple flames flickering in the folds of fabric.

And behind her, creeping up the crooked trail, was a shadowy, shaggy form! "Look out!" screeched Lewis in alarm.

Mrs. Zimmermann whirled. The shadow-creature suddenly reared, its arms spread wide in menace, its glowering yellow eyes flashing. Lewis saw Mrs. Zimmermann push Rose Rita behind her. Facing the wavery monster, she took step after step backward up the hillside. Finally she stepped into the circle around the tower. The horrible shape came right up to the edge of the circle and then started to prowl the edge, like a hungry jungle beast.

"We're safe as long as we don't go outside the circle," said Jonathan. "But why didn't that creature vanish when it took Izard? A wizard's spells usually end when he dies!"

"Remember, he's got lots of other wicked sorcerers helping him," replied Mrs. Zimmermann. She cast a despairing gaze upward. "Less than two minutes!" she said. "Have you found the clock?"

"No," said Jonathan. "Help us look!"

Rose Rita yanked her gaze off the shadow-beast and said, "Maybe it's hidden somewhere really obvious, like the purloined letter in the Edgar Allan Poe story. Could it be in one of those awful sculptures? In one of the crystal skulls, or—"

Lewis looked back up the hill. In the single patch of sunlight the shadow of the tower had shrunk to a very small dark pool. The shadow cast by the spire was almost touching the twelve spears—

And then he had it!

"It's a sundial!" he screamed. "The whole hill is a sundial! We can't see the clock because *we're standing right on top of it!*" He pointed at the shadow of the spire. "When that touches the twelve—and there are twelve of those spears—the sun will go out and the spell will begin!"

"Oh, my Lord," said Mrs. Zimmermann. "You're right! Stand back, everyone!"

She pointed her wand at the top of the tower. She quickly recited a spell in ancient Gothic, and from the tip of her wand, a purple lightning bolt shot out. It arced through the air and slammed into the roof of the tower. With a furious explosion, the stones flew apart and the spire toppled. "Get back!" shouted Jonathan. He hooked one arm around Lewis's waist and one around Rose Rita and dragged them away.

Lewis winced. The whole top of the tower roof had been blasted off. It whistled to earth and struck not three feet away from Mrs. Zimmermann. The spire impaled itself in the ground. The clouds, which had been whirling faster and faster, suddenly boiled. From all around them rose a shriek louder than anything Lewis had ever heard. He clapped his hands over his ears.

The crystal skulls exploded, one after the other, with reports as loud as a shotgun being fired! The steel spears melted like licorice over a hot stove! The metal bats caught fire and blazed with a blinding white light! And the tower began to heave and rumble. Stones fell from the flying buttress that supported the steps!

"Run, Florence!" yelled Jonathan. "Kids, get to the boat!"

"I won't leave Mrs. Zimmermann!" insisted Rose Rita. She wormed out of Jonathan's grasp and ran to her friend. Mrs. Zimmermann turned, her eyes wide and dazed. She stumbled, and then Rose Rita was beside her. She threw Mrs. Zimmermann's arm around her shoulder and began to walk her toward the pathway.

The marble tombstones had become something cobwebby. They wavered, then blew away in sickly gray streamers. Lewis staggered as the ground under his feet heaved. It was like trying to walk across a gigantic squishy mattress. The whole island was gurgling. Trees were sinking into the earth as if they stood on quicksand.

And there, shaking and swelling, stood the shadow-creature! It blocked the path. Jonathan looked at Mrs. Zimmermann. Then he said, "I suppose this has to be up to me. Here's hoping I've got what it takes!"

Lewis felt sick. Jonathan strode out of the circle and the shadow surged forward, stretching toward him. With his feet wide apart Jonathan held his cane straight before him. In a voice like thunder he cried out, *"Lux et veritas!"*

Blinding light blossomed from the crystal globe on his cane! Lewis saw it strike the shadow-monster and lift it into the air. Streamers of light pierced and shredded it, pieces of shadow whirling away into nothingness!

And it was gone!

Turning, Jonathan grabbed Mrs. Zimmermann's free arm. Only then did Lewis notice that her staff had become an umbrella again, a plain black umbrella with a crystal globe for the handle. "I'm all right," whispered Mrs. Zimmermann. "Just wasn't prepared for the whammy! 'Light and Truth,' Jonathan? Pretty nifty spell for a parlor magician! Let's go!"

They stumbled down the heaving path and passed the cottage, which was glistening sickly like the slime from slugs and seeping into the ground. Lewis looked over his shoulder. So many trees had been sucked into the earth that he could see the tower. It was moving, reeling, and shedding black stones. Then with a terribly loud *snap!* that sounded like the crack of doom, it broke and fell.

Lewis screamed in alarm. The path had become liquid, like horrible, thick mud. He felt himself sinking in it up to his knees. Everyone around him was floundering and falling. But just ahead was the pier, and Izard's boat and their own.

With a superhuman effort, Jonathan, who had sunk into the mud up to his waist, picked Lewis up. "Here you go!" he exclaimed, and Lewis felt himself being tossed through the air. He shouted in alarm, and then plunged into cold water! Fighting his way to the surface, he grabbed something solid—the gunwale of Jonathan's boat! He flopped over the rail and into the boat. Ahead of him, the waters of Lake Superior were reclaiming Gnomon Island. Uncle Jonathan was holding Rose Rita up, and beside him, Mrs. Zimmermann reeled with one hand on his shoulder. Both of them had sunk into the soft earth, but now the water was washing around their waists.

"Hang on!" screamed Lewis. He snatched the mooring lines and yanked, and they tore the cleats right out of the nearly liquid wood of the pier. Lewis grabbed one of the pier supports and pushed hard. It was nasty, like plunging his hand into something so rotten, it had turned greasy and soft, but the effort made the boat drift. Jonathan surged ahead one step, two steps, and then he was at the edge of the boat. He lifted Rose Rita in and tossed his cane after her. Then, even as he sank in up to his chest, he boosted Mrs. Zimmermann in. "Go!" he bellowed. "I'll be all right! Take her out, Lewis!"

Mrs. Zimmermann, panting for breath, threw herself flat and grabbed one of Jonathan's arms. "I've got him!" she said. "Start the engine!"

Lewis yanked the cord. The outboard coughed once, then fired up. "Hold on tight!" he roared. He turned the nose of the boat as slowly as he dared, and they began to pull away from the island, with Uncle Jonathan desperately clinging to the boat and to Mrs. Zimmermann.

"Look at that," said Rose Rita in a voice filled with awe. Lewis chanced a look back. The whole island was dissolving. It ran down into the water of the lake like a putrid mass. And overhead, the clouds were thinning and breaking up.

"Let me get in!" yelled Uncle Jonathan. Rose Rita and Lewis leaned way back as he came slopping and slipping over the side, bringing about half of Lake Superior in with him. He was shaking. "So much for the Doomsday Clock," he growled. "There it goes! The whole island's going to drip away."

"And 'leave not a wrack behind,'" said Mrs. Zimmermann, quoting from Shakespeare's *The Tempest*. "But did we destroy the Doomsday Clock in time? Did we kill the spell, or did—"

She didn't finish. But Lewis knew what she couldn't bear to say: "Or did the spell kill everyone else?"

CHAPTER FIFTEEN

Lewis soon found, to his relief, that they had been in time. Although Grampa Galway said there had been some "mighty strange weather," nothing terrible had happened. But more than a week passed before he found out the rest of the story.

That came on a warm summer night back in New Zebedee. They were all back, even Grampa Galway, whose friend had returned from Australia with a gold cup for having won his yacht race. But he wasn't in the backyard of 100 High Street when Mrs. Zimmermann told Jonathan, Rose Rita, and Lewis what she had learned.

"Professor Athanasius and the others think that we really hurled a monkey wrench into the world of evil magic," she said with a smile. "We probably will never know how many magicians had signed on with Ishmael

Izard in his mad plan for world domination. There were certainly hundreds. Maybe a thousand or more. But from what my friends from all over the world tell me, their magic has been completely drained. They couldn't turn cream into butter with what they have left! Some of them are awfully angry with old Droopy Drawers. If they could find him—well, maybe the creatures of shadow were easier on him than his friends would have been!"

Jonathan nodded. "I thought something like that would happen. Ishmael was calling on a lot of power to keep that island together and solid. When Florence snapped off the pointer to the sundial, everything sort of backfired. When the island dissolved, it took their power right along with it!"

Rose Rita breathed out a sigh of relief. "Then the world is safe."

Mrs. Zimmermann's eyes twinkled. "Well—safe from the last of the Izards, anyway! And with all of those evil sorcerers defanged, it will be safer and more comfortable in lots of other ways. Still, you have to remember that not every bad magician in the world joined forces with Ishmael. We still have to keep our guard up." She turned to Jonathan and said, "By the way, Frazzle Face, I didn't break the tip off any 'pointer.' I have found out that the official name for the doojigger that casts a shadow on the face of a sundial is *gnomon*."

Jonathan slapped his forehead. "Gnomon Island! Oh, my gosh! Now I wish I'd paid attention to all those vocabulary quizzes in English class!"

With a sheepish smile Mrs. Zimmermann said, "The

clock was so big, we couldn't see it. Just counting those spooky sculptures should have tipped us off. They were the hours of the day, from six in the morning to six in the evening!"

Jonathan shook his head. Then he fished in his vest pocket. "Oh, by the way, Florence, I took care of this." He handed her a slip of paper.

She took it suspiciously and read it. Then she laughed. "You paid for my rental boat!" she said. "Seven hundred dollars! I'll pay you back."

"No need," said Jonathan with a smile. "I think we got off cheap at the price! And I can well afford it. I just told the owner that you'd cracked the boat up and it sank like a stone."

"I'm a better driver than that!" scolded Mrs. Zimmermann, but she was grinning.

For a few moments no one spoke. Then Lewis hesitantly asked, "Are you going to be all right, Mrs. Zimmermann? I mean, you didn't drain all of *your* power or anything, did you? You looked pretty—"

"Pretty much like something the cat dragged in?" Mrs. Zimmermann finished. "I don't wonder! No, my magic is perfectly fine, thank you very much. But, my heavens! Snapping that spell gave me a nasty moment or two. I felt as if I'd grabbed hold of a live wire. I'm just lucky that Rose Rita and Jonathan are so stubborn. I don't think I could have found my way down to the dock without them tugging and shoving me along!"

"You're very welcome, Haggy," Jonathan replied. "And anyway, you more than paid me back by hanging on to my arm while the island was trying to drag me down with it!" He cracked his knuckles. "Now then, speaking of magic . . . I know that Lewis always likes historical battles, but tonight I thought I'd try a spell that's just a bit different. Since we saved the human race and gave it a future, I thought I might conjure up a nice little illusion for us to play in. Ready?"

It took some doing, but when at last his preparations were over, Jonathan waved his walking stick and intoned a spell. A pink mist swirled in, and when it settled, they were standing on a rusty-red hillside that was covered with snow. The sun seemed faint and shrunken, and the sky was pink. Farther away in the distance, Lewis could see some domes and the green smudge of growing things. "Where are we?" he asked.

His uncle laughed. "On Mars, of course! But not Mars as it is today—Mars as it will be hundreds of years in the future, when humans have made it more Earthlike and have colonized it. And here's the best part: Mars has very low gravity!"

With a sudden bound, Jonathan jumped straight into the sky. He soared up for ten or fifteen feet, then came gracefully back to—well, not Earth, but to the ground. "Try it!" he said. "It's loads of fun!"

Soon Rose Rita and Lewis were bounding and leaping this way and that, laughing their heads off. It was like being on the greatest trampoline in the universe. Uncle Jonathan stood with his hands on his hips, beaming. "What could be more fun than this?" he asked.

Whap! He yelped as a soft snowball burst against his

head. He spun around and saw Mrs. Zimmermann balling up another one.

"What could be more fun?" she asked mischievously. "A good old-fashioned futuristic snowball fight, of course!"

Rose Rita and Lewis settled back down to watch Jonathan and Mrs. Zimmermann whooping and tossing Martian snowballs back and forth. Lewis started to giggle. So did Rose Rita. Then they were both roaring. The peals of their laughter rose high into the strange sky of Mars. It was a good sound.